SHIPMENT ONE

Tex Times Ten by Tina Leonard
Runaway Cowboy by Judy Christenberry
Crazy for Lovin' You by Teresa Southwick
The Rancher Next Door by Cathy Gillen Thacker
Intimate Secrets by B.J. Daniels
Operation: Texas by Roxanne Rustand

SHIPMENT TWO

Navarro or Not by Tina Leonard
Trust a Cowboy by Judy Christenberry
Taming a Dark Horse by Stella Bagwell
The Rancher's Family Thanksgiving by Cathy Gillen Thacker
The Valentine Two-Step by RaeAnne Thayne
The Cowboy and the Bride by Marin Thomas

SHIPMENT THREE

Catching Calhoun by Tina Leonard
The Christmas Cowboy by Judy Christenberry
The Come-Back Cowboy by Jodi O'Donnell
The Rancher's Christmas Baby by Cathy Gillen Thacker
Baby Love by Victoria Pade
The Best Catch in Texas by Stella Bagwell
This Kiss by Teresa Southwick

SHIPMENT FOUR

Archer's Angels by Tina Leonard
More to Texas than Cowboys by Roz Denny Fox
The Rancher's Promise by Jodi O'Donnell
The Gentleman Rancher by Cathy Gillen Thacker
Cowboy's Baby by Victoria Pade
Having the Cowboy's Baby by Stella Bagwell

SHIPMENT FIVE

Belonging to Bandera by Tina Leonard
Court Me, Cowboy by Barbara White Daille
His Best Friend's Bride by Jodi O'Donnell
The Cowboy's Return by Linda Warren
Baby Be Mine by Victoria Pade
The Cattle Baron by Margaret Way

SHIPMENT SIX

Crockett's Seduction by Tina Leonard
Coming Home to the Cattleman by Judy Christenberry
Almost Perfect by Judy Duarte
Cowboy Dad by Cathy McDavid
Real Cowboys by Roz Denny Fox
The Rancher Wore Suits by Rita Herron
Falling for the Texas Tycoon by Karen Rose Smith

SHIPMENT SEVEN

Last's Temptation by Tina Leonard
Daddy by Choice by Marin Thomas
The Cowboy, the Baby and the Bride-to-Be by Cara Colter
Luke's Proposal by Lois Faye Dyer
The Truth About Cowboys by Margot Early
The Other Side of Paradise by Laurie Paige

SHIPMENT EIGHT

Mason's Marriage by Tina Leonard
Bride at Briar's Ridge by Margaret Way
Texas Bluff by Linda Warren
Cupid and the Cowboy by Carol Finch
The Horseman's Son by Delores Fossen
Cattleman's Bride-to-Be by Lois Faye Dyer

The rugged, masculine and independent men
of America's West know the value of hard work,
honor and family. They may be ranchers, tycoons
or the guy next door, but they're all cowboys at heart.
Don't miss any of the books in this collection!

Cowboy
at
Heart

HAVING THE
COWBOY'S BABY

STELLA BAGWELL

USA TODAY Bestselling Author

HARLEQUIN® COWBOY AT HEART

Recycling programs
for this product may
not exist in your area.

ISBN-13: 978-0-373-82625-4

HAVING THE COWBOY'S BABY

Printed in U.S.A.

STELLA BAGWELL

has written more than seventy novels for Harlequin and Silhouette Books. She credits her loyal readers and hopes her stories have brightened their lives in some small way.

A cowgirl through and through, she loves to watch old Westerns, and has recently learned how to rope a steer. Her days begin and end helping her husband care for a beloved herd of horses on their little ranch located on the south Texas coast. When she's not ropin' and ridin', you'll find her at her desk, creating her next tale of love. The couple have a son, who is a high school math teacher and athletic coach. Stella loves to hear from readers and invites them to contact her at stellabagwell@gmail.com.

To all my readers.
Thank you from the bottom of my heart.

Chapter One

Oh God, don't let it happen again.

Anne-Marie Duveuil refused to fall under the spell of a man like Cordero Sanchez. She'd already had her life's plan of entering a convent shattered by one sexy man. To let another one turn her head would be worse than a sin, it would be ruination.

She'd never met anyone with such rakish features or such a sexual presence. His hair was crow-black and waved to the back of his neck in a length that was far too long to be neat. But then, neat wouldn't match a man like him, she decided. He was a rebel and a rounder. Even though he'd not said one word out of place since he'd arrived, she could see trouble all over his handsome face and long lean body. And she desperately wished that anyone other than this man had delivered her father's newly acquired horses to Cane's Landing.

A few minutes ago Anne-Marie had shown her guest into the parlor for refreshments. After all, he'd traveled a long distance to get here and her mother had taught her to be a proper hostess, even when a visitor made her feel uncomfortable. And Cordero Sanchez was definitely doing that and much more.

Up to this point she'd tried her best to keep their conversation polite and impersonal, but the man seemed dead set on learning about her family's history. A moment ago he'd left his chair to inspect the long row of photos resting on the rock mantle of the fireplace and innate manners had forced Anne-Marie to cross the room to stand by his side.

"That's my father when he was a very young man," she explained as he paused to examine one particular photo. "In those days he liked to hunt ducks and the bird dogs you see with him were some that he'd trained."

"I didn't know that Jules liked to hunt," he admitted. "But then we're always talking horses."

Forsaking the image of her father, he moved on down the hearth and she stiffened as he picked up an enlarged snapshot of her. In it she was wearing a simple yellow sundress and her long hair was tied back with a coral colored scarf. Several young children with brown skin and black hair were standing with her in front of a crude, clapboard building.

"That was in Guatemala," she said quietly. "I was teaching at a Catholic school."

He looked at her with open interest. "You're a teacher?"

A negligible shrug barely moved her shoulder. "I taught languages for a while. But that was long ago, when I still had dreams of entering a convent."

Clearly stunned by her revelation, she could feel him staring at her.

"A convent!" He repeated the word with hushed amazement. "What happened?"

As she lifted her eyes to his, her lips twisted to a bitter line. "I met a man just like you."

An expression of comical confusion swept across his dark face. "What the hell does that mean?"

Flustered with him and herself, her cheeks began to burn.

Her cheeks still burning, she exclaimed, "Oh! I shouldn't have said that. I'm sorry, Cordero."

His hazel-green eyes continued to study her closely. "It's all right. But I got the impression that this…man you just compared me to is not someone on your most valued list."

"No." Turning away from him, she walked over to the coffee table and returned her glass to the tray of cold refreshments that Darcella, their cook, had provided for them. "But that has nothing to do with you." Keeping her back to him, she added, "I mean. Not personally. He just happened to be a man that was virile and handsome, like you. That's all."

Cordero had never had trouble garnering attention from the opposite sex, but he'd never been stuck on himself. When he looked in the mirror he saw a regular guy, a horseman who did his best to enjoy every minute of the day. To hear this vision of a woman call him virile and handsome jolted him.

"What was this man to you?" Cordero asked thoughtfully.

She looked at him then, her face full of wry resignation. "He was my lover."

If she'd walked over and slapped him hard on the face he wouldn't have been any more floored. He could say nothing. At least nothing that would make sense. Yet she seemed to be waiting for some sort of reply, so he drew in a deep breath and said the first thing that came to his mind. "I take it things didn't work out."

"No."

Cordero wished she would tell him more, but he wasn't going to prod her. Even if he did kick up his heels on Saturday night with the rest of the wranglers on his family's ranch, he liked to think of himself as a gentleman. And since he'd only arrived at this Louisiana sugar cane plantation an hour ago, he could hardly start prying into the woman's personal life. But he had to admit that he fervently wanted to.

He'd never seen a woman quite so beautiful. Oh, he'd seen plenty of glamour girls, but they were mostly paint and powder and provocative clothing. This woman was nothing close to that. Her blue eyes were like chunks of crystal sky and her bare lips the soft pink of a wild rose. A glow that had nothing to do with the heat of the summer afternoon seemed to emanate from her pearly skin. She was as natural and as breathtaking as the rising sun.

She cleared her throat and smiled as though the two of them had just been discussing the weather instead of her ex-lover. The abrupt change jarred him. But not any more than learning when he'd arrived that his old friend Jules Duveuil had a young, beautiful daughter.

"It's getting late," she observed with a glance at her watch. "If you're ready, maybe we should head to the hospital."

To add to Cordero's surprise, he'd also learned that Jules had been admitted to a hospital in Thibodaux only yesterday. Three days before Cordero had left Texas, he'd spoken with the older man over the phone and nothing had been amiss then. Jules had sounded healthy and excited that Cordero would soon be arriving with the pair of gray quarter horses from the Sandbur ranch.

Apparently Jules had a heart condition and the doctor had admitted him for a few tests. Now the old man was asking to see Cordero and he couldn't refuse. Jules Duveuil had been a friend to Cordero and his family for more than two years.

Cordero had first met Jules at a cutting horse show in Houston and since then Jules had sent several horse buyers to the ranch, who'd spent thousands of dollars on Sandbur horses. Only a month ago, Jules had flown down to the south Texas ranch to view their quarter horses. He'd purchased a pair without any quibbling over the price. There was no way Cordero could slight Jules by avoiding a visit to the hospital. In Cordero's opinion, the older man was more than a good client; he was a friend.

Nodding his agreement at Anne-Marie, Cordero stepped past her and retrieved his hat from the floor where he'd left it at the foot of an armchair. As he pulled the brim down on his forehead, he said, "Yeah, let's get going. I'm anxious to see your father."

In the front room, she gathered her handbag from a small table, then headed toward the door. Cordero automatically followed while his mind spun. From the first moment he'd spotted Anne-Marie walking across the yard to greet him, he'd been totally mesmerized by the sight of her. She'd been dressed in some sort of gauzy white dress that floated around her slender body like a thin misty cloud. Flaming copper hair had hung in thick waves to the middle of her back and caressed the faint jut of her breasts. Even from a distance, he'd been able to see that her skin was milky white and as smooth as top cream. As she'd walked toward him there'd been a smile on her face that had made him think of a Southern belle hiding her expression behind a palmetto fan. Now that she'd confessed to a broken romance and diverted plans to enter a convent, she was even more intriguing. What sort of man had seduced her, he wondered, and why wasn't she with him now?

Careful, Cordero, don't try to make this woman your business. She's not for you. Not

even close. You want those carefree, love
'em and leave 'em types. Not a sweet angel
with a broken wing.

"We'll take my car," she said once they
were out on the porch. "That way you won't
have to worry with unhitching your horse
trailer."

"It's really no problem if you'd like for
me to drive my truck," he offered.

"That isn't necessary. My car is parked
right over here in the garage."

The Duveuil house wasn't the typical
Grecian structure he'd expected to find at
Cane's Landing. Instead of typical white
pillars and redbrick, the massive two-story
was made entirely of wood and displayed a
Creole flavor. Verandahs, with overhangs
supported by carved black posts, lined all
sides of the structure. Matching black shutters bracketed the many windows on the
graceful facade.

As he followed Anne-Marie down the
front steps, he noticed that live oaks, all of
them dripping with Spanish moss, hugged
the house with massive sagging limbs.
Along the lattice-covered foundation, dahl-

ias, camellias and hollyhocks bloomed bright and lush.

The estate was beautiful, he silently noted, but compared to the Sandbur ranch it was damn quiet. Back in Texas there were always people and vehicles about, cowboys and cattle buyers milling around the barns and pens. Here at Cane's Landing the only sounds he'd heard were the songbirds and an occasional bark from a bluetick hound.

The garage was a separate building situated about a hundred feet from the house. Presently the double doors were opened and he could see a dark green luxury car parked on the left side.

She handed him the keys. "I hate driving," she said. "Will you do the chore?"

For her? Cordero would split a cord of wood with an ax or stack ten ton of hay in the barn loft just to see a tiny smile on her face. Merely looking at her made him feel like an adolescent and he didn't know how to deal with his strange reaction. It was downright scary. He needed to get away from Cane's Landing just as fast as he could get. But how the heck was he going to do that, when he'd already promised Jules he'd spend the remainder of the week here?

But he'd made that promise before he'd met Jules's beautiful daughter. Now he had to find some way to cut short his stay. Otherwise, this vision with flaming hair was going to end up leading him around by the nose. And he wasn't the sort of man to let himself be led by a woman.

"I'd be glad to drive," he told her.

After helping her into the passenger seat, he walked around the car and slid beneath the steering wheel. The seat squished comfortably around him like a marshmallow.

There was no doubt the Duveuils' finances were secure. If this woman ever did look at him in a man-to-woman way, it wouldn't be for his money. They were equal in that aspect, but polar opposites in every other way. He couldn't see Anne-Marie at a Texas dance hall, kicking up her heels in a pair of jeans and cowboy boots. No more than he could imagine himself joining her on a missionary trek to some third world country. Those differences ought to be enough to make him keep his hands to himself. Still, it wasn't enough to stop the itch to touch her.

Slowly, he eased the car down the oak-lined lane. Once they had reached the black-topped road, Anne-Marie instructed him to turn left. With the setting of the sun, the massive pines sent deep shadows across the roadway and made the evening seem much older than it was. The dimness of the car interior cocooned them together. As the miles passed, Cordero found his gaze slipping over to her slim figure far more than safety allowed.

He needed to keep his mind on the job of driving rather than on her. But she was a tempting sight and the clothes she'd changed into made looking at her even more pleasant. Her beige slacks were slim-fitting linen and matched the short, sleeveless top that left her arms and a provocative amount of skin at the neckline exposed to his view. It would be easy enough to reach across the seat and slide a finger against that soft skin, but he figured her response would be fast and furious.

Realizing he needed to break the train of his thoughts, Cordero asked, "What does your father plan to do with the horses? Since I've run into him at several horse shows here lately, I thought he might be planning to ride himself."

Anne-Marie continued to stare out the window. It was much safer and wiser than looking at him. "It's been several years since we've had horses here at Cane's Landing. Father's only started going to horse shows again after his health forced him to retire from managing the plantation. I guess the competition never left his blood, but now it's not for himself. It's for me."

"You?"

There was so much surprise in his voice that she turned to look at him. He was staring at her in disbelief and the sight nettled her in a way she'd not felt in years. Just because he was from Texas didn't mean he was an expert on equines or who was qualified to ride them.

"Why, yes. I do ride. And I have since I was a very young girl." Folding her hands together on her lap, she silently told herself to relax. This man's opinion of her was of no importance. His stay here would be short. Besides, it wasn't his fault that he had enough sexuality for ten men and that she was too weak-willed to ignore it.

Breathing deeply, she added, "Father wants me to compete in Western reining or in cutting competitions. But I'm not sure I want to do either."

Cordero couldn't imagine this woman even sitting astride a horse, much less riding one as it spun in tight circles or jumped violently back and forth to head off a cantankerous steer. But then he'd been surprised by women before. In fact, most of them were never what they appeared to be on the surface. He was beginning to think Anne-Marie wasn't what she appeared to be, either.

"Why not?" he asked. "You don't have the confidence to compete?"

She started to take offense at his question, before she realized he was asking it sincerely.

"Well, I'm not timid," she answered. "And I'm sure I could get my riding skills sharpened fairly quickly. But that's not the issue. I have...other plans that have nothing to do with horses."

"Apparently your father doesn't know about your 'other' plans."

Her mouth pressed into a grim line. "Oh yes, he does. But he's the persistent type. He'll never give up on the idea of me following his wishes instead of mine."

Cordero couldn't help but wonder if her "other" plans had anything to do with a man. But he quickly told himself to forget the question. Anne-Marie wasn't the modern, free-spirited sort. She was the picture of old-fashioned family values. She'd even wanted to enter a convent! If she ever did decide to get involved with a man, it would be with marriage in mind. And matrimony, with any woman, was not part of Cordero's plans. He'd seen too much loss, too much heartache, in his family to risk putting himself through such pain.

Seven years ago, his brother's wife had died in a tragic riding accident, then Cordero's mother had died from health problems in the very same year, leaving their father a grieving husband. After that, Cordero had helplessly watched both men struggle to deal with the emptiness. He'd vowed then that he wouldn't suffer like that. Love just wasn't worth the heartache. Since that time he'd stuck to his promise.

In a matter of moments, the outskirts of town appeared and Anne-Marie gave Cordero directions to the hospital. Since the small town was easy to navigate, they were soon entering the building and riding the elevator up to her father's room.

"Does your father know we're coming?" he asked as they made their way down a long corridor.

"I promised I'd get you here as soon as we got the horses settled. I'm sure he's expecting us at any time." She regarded him thoughtfully. "I hope being in a hospital doesn't upset you. Some people can't deal with illness and death. If you're uncomfortable just tell me and we'll make the visit as short as we can."

Cordero shook his head. "I don't look at a hospital as a bad place to be. My father just went through a very serious operation. He was paralyzed, now he's almost back to normal. I thank God for these places."

She seemed surprised by his comment, but then she quickly smiled. "I'm glad you feel that way, Cordero."

The way she said his name, with that Cajun lilt, did something to him. Each time it rolled past her lips, he felt his stomach turn over. He couldn't imagine what it would do to him if she whispered in his ear, murmuring his name with longing.

"Here it is," she said, gesturing toward the next door to their right.

Her announcement jolted him out of the half trance he'd sunk into. As the two of them entered the hospital room, he cleared his throat and lifted his hat from his head.

The small space was typical of a hospital. The spare utilitarian bed was raised at the head, while a television with the sound muted was mounted to the ceiling in one corner of the room. Jules Duveuil, dressed in a thin maroon robe over matching pajamas, was sitting in a padded vinyl chair with his feet propped on a footstool. Small reading glasses perched on the end of his nose, while the front section of the *Times-Picayune* was on his lap. He had thick gray hair and a slim, aristocratic face. Cordero never had been good at guessing people's ages, but he figured Anne-Marie's father had passed seventy and then some. His condition couldn't be terribly serious, Cordero hoped, because he wasn't hooked up to an IV or oxygen.

The moment Jules spotted the two of them, his face brightened and he smiled with pleasure.

"Finally! I've been expecting you all evening," he exclaimed.

Quickly leaving Cordero's side, Anne-Marie kissed her father's wrinkled cheek.

"I'm sorry. It took us a while to get the horses settled." Rising to her full height, she gestured toward Cordero. "Mr. Sanchez was sorry to hear you were in the hospital."

"Forget the Mr. Sanchez thing. I know him by Cordero." Grinning broadly, Jules extended his hand. "Glad you're finally here, son. Thank you for coming."

Cordero walked over to Jules and gave the older man's hand a firm shake. "No thanks necessary. I just hope you're feeling better."

Jules batted a hand at the air in a dismissive gesture. "Oh, it's nothing really. I think the doctors have decided they can't kill me with the stuff they've been making me swallow so they're trying something new."

Anne-Marie rolled her eyes and groaned. "Oh, Father, don't make a joke about your health."

Jules shot Cordero a conspiring wink before he said to his daughter. "Honey, we're all mortal. It's not something we can change or buy our way out of. When my time comes, nothing, especially all this fretting you're doing, will stop it and neither can these know-it-all doctors. The best a person can do is to have fun until you reach that time."

"Jules, I couldn't have said that any better," Cordero replied with a grin.

His blue eyes twinkling, Jules cast his daughter a smug smile. "See, my young friend knows a little about life." He gave Cordero an appreciative look. "I want to thank you again for all the trouble you've taken by bringing my horses home. How did they make the trip?"

"Fine, Jules. No problems. We put them in the round pen for tonight so they could get a little exercise. Were you planning to keep them stalled or put them out to pasture?"

Jules looked at his daughter with mild surprise. "You didn't show him the trap?"

Anne-Marie looked as though she wanted to sigh with frustration. Maybe the two of them had quarreled openly about the purchase of the horses. She'd already admitted that she wasn't keen on Jules's idea that she should ride competitively. The last thing Cordero wanted was to get in the middle of a family squabble.

"No," she said. "I didn't go into all of that. Mr. Sanchez, uh, Cordero arrived rather late. I'll show him the area tomorrow and see if he thinks it will be adequate." She looked at Cordero and quickly explained. "The trap Father is talking about is a small, two-acre pasture not far from the stables."

Cordero nodded. "I'll look it over before I leave tomorrow."

Jules began to splutter. "Leave? You're not planning on leaving tomorrow, are you?"

Trying not to feel guilty, Cordero said, "Well, yes. Now that you're laid up in the hospital, we can't go to that horse sale up in Bossier City or do the other things we'd planned to do. I need to get out of the way and let you get well."

His lips compressed with disapproval, Jules motioned for Anne-Marie to fetch the empty plastic chair sitting near the head of the bed. "Get our guest a seat," he said.

Cordero grabbed the chair before Anne-Marie could do the old man's bidding. But rather than taking the chair for himself, he took her by the arm and urged her onto the seat. "I'm fine standing. You sit, Anne-Marie."

While she murmured her thanks and made herself comfortable, he straightened to his full height. Jules was regarding him in a thoughtful, almost conspiring way.

"All right, Cordero. Now what's all this talk about leaving tomorrow? I know this hospital thing has thrown a few kinks in our plans but there's no need for you to cut your visit short. Even though I can't get out and about, Anne-Marie can. In fact, this may be the perfect time for you to help my daughter get accustomed to being back in the saddle."

From the corner of his eye Cordero could see Anne-Marie close her eyes with embarrassment. Cordero shuffled his weight from one boot to the other. "Uh, I'm not really into the instructing part of things. Now my father—"

"Isn't here," Jules interrupted. "You are."

"Father," Anne-Marie spoke up in a slightly scolding tone, "Cordero is a busy man. He has a ranch to take care of. He didn't come all the way to Louisiana to give me riding lessons!"

Jules leveled a gentle smile at his daughter. "Anne-Marie would you be a sweetheart and go get your father a cup of coffee? You know how I like it, with cream and sugar."

Clearly annoyed with him, she frowned. "Why don't you just say you want to talk to Cordero without my presence? Wouldn't that have been easier?"

Jules looked up at Cordero and gestured to Anne-Marie with a fond smile. "Stubborn redhead—just like her mother was." To Anne-Marie, he said, "All right, daughter. I want to speak to our guest in private. But I do want the coffee, too. Is that better?"

For a moment Cordero thought she might argue, but then with the tiniest of sighs, she rose from the chair and left the room.

Once the door had shut behind her, Jules leaned earnestly forward in his chair.

"Okay, now that my daughter is out of listening range, I'll say this flat out. I'll pay you anything you ask if you'll agree to stick around for the remainder of the week."

Cordero was beginning to feel extremely uncomfortable. This request wasn't about horses and a friendship between two men. It would be crazy for him to get involved. But there was such a desperate look on Jules's face that Cordero didn't have the heart to give the man an absolute no. He owed him too much.

"Hell, Jules, I didn't agree to stay at Cane's Landing to take on the job of riding instructor! And I don't want any sort of pay! I thought you and I were going to—"

Jules held up his hand. "I know we'd planned to do a lot of things together while you're here in Louisiana. But that's off. And now I'm asking a favor from you. If you don't want pay for it, that's fine—even better."

Cordero let out a long breath. "I don't think your daughter wants my help."

Jules features twisted into a sardonic expression. "Anne-Marie has never known what the hell she wants. That bastard in her past ruined her. Or so she thinks. She sees herself as spoiled goods. She was always so virtuous before him. And then after she fell for him—well, she's hidden from life. Now she's secluded herself at Cane's Landing, telling herself that her father needs her constant attention."

"And you don't?"

Jules swatted the air with his hand and muttered another curse. "No. And I'll confess to you, Cordero, I'm only here in the hospital because I made my doctor put me here!"

Stunned by this revelation, Cordero sank into the seat Anne-Marie had vacated. "How did you manage to do that?"

"Threatened to take away all my donations to the hospital fund," he said smugly. "Money will do it every time."

Cordero's head swung back and forth as he tried to get the whole picture. "I don't understand. Why do you want to be in this place?" Glancing around the room, Cordero figured he'd have to have a mighty good reason to be cloistered in such a place if it wasn't necessary. "And why drag me into this?"

Jules looked as if he considered Cordero to be as slow as molasses on a cold morning. "Because I knew you were bringing the horses and if I'd been home, Anne-Marie would have stayed hidden in her room and let me deal with you and the animals. Me being out of the house forces her to act like she's alive. Now I need to stay in here a few days longer—until you're able to get her into the saddle and her mind on something else besides—"

"Besides what? Has your daughter had some sort of health problem or something?"

The old man's mouth snapped shut and he looked at Cordero for several long, thoughtful moments. "Look, Cordero, my daughter is too good for her own good. She never thinks about herself, only others. She's wasting her youth—hiding herself because she's afraid to deal with real life. I bought the horses hoping she'd be interested in something that would get her away from the plantation. I think someone like you could nudge her into it if you'd just give her a little push. I know you like a son. You come from a good family and I trust you with my daughter."

What did Cordero look like? A psychologist in cowboy boots? He was feeling more awkward by the minute. Especially since Anne-Marie had more or less told him that she wanted her own life, not the one her father wanted for her.

"It sounds like what you want for your daughter is a companion. And I can't be that, Jules. Not even for a week. It wouldn't be right."

The old man's eyes narrowed perceptively. "You've told me before that you weren't married. Have you gotten engaged or something?"

Cordero had to stifle a groan. "No. And I damn well don't plan to. But that's not the point."

Relief, or something close to it, crossed Jules face. "Good," he said with a smile. "You'd already planned to take some time off from the Sandbur. You can think of the next few days as a vacation."

Las Vegas would be a vacation, Cordero thought. Bright lights. Music and gambling tables. Beautiful, scantily dressed showgirls. That was his idea of fun. Not a plantation where the most action he was likely to see was a hound treeing a squirrel. And yet, he had to admit that the thought of spending more time with Anne-Marie was an enticing notion. She might present a prim appearance on the outside, but she wasn't completely innocent on the inside. She'd already admitted that she'd had a lover. If Cordero played his cards right, he might persuade her that a brief tryst with him would be perfectly harmless. And giving the beautiful redhead a few instructions in bed would be far more enjoyable than giving her riding lessons.

He glanced thoughtfully at Jules. Here he was making plans to seduce his good friend's daughter. Did that mean he was betraying Jules's trust? Of course not.

Hell, Cordero thought, he shouldn't even let that question cross his mind. Not when Jules was handing over his daughter on a silver platter.

"All right, Jules," Cordero said after a moment. "I'll stay. For a day or two. If by then Anne-Marie doesn't seem to resent me being around, I'll wait until Sunday to leave for Texas."

Today was Monday, Cordero silently calculated. That would give him six days with Anne-Marie. A shrewd smile crossed his face. In that length of time, he could make most anything happen.

Chapter Two

Slapping his knee, Jules beamed. "I couldn't ask any more than that from you, son. And I won't forget this. I'll pay the favor back. You can bet on that."

This was looking more and more like an attempt at matchmaking. Admitting himself into the hospital and asking a friend to keep his daughter company wasn't a normal request from a father. But whatever Jules had planned, it originated in the love he had for his daughter.

"You've already done enough for me, Jules. And don't thank me yet. Anne-Marie isn't a pushover. If she isn't interested in the horses, I can't twist her arm."

Jules snorted. "If she isn't interested in the horses, then get her interested in you! The girl needs her temperature raised a little and I don't care how you do it."

Before Cordero could make any response to the old man's remark, a swishing noise sounded behind him. Cordero glanced over his shoulder to see Anne-Marie pushing through the door. The foam cup she carried was steaming.

"One of the nurses just made a new pot, so it should be fresh," she told him.

With a tender smile for his daughter, Jules took the coffee from her. "You're the best, sweetheart." He took a careful sip and his eyes twinkled as he gave Anne-Marie another big smile. "And I have good news for you. Cordero has agreed to stay on with us for a few days—just like he first planned."

With a stunned expression, she whipped her head around to stare at Cordero. "You— you're not going home tomorrow after all?"

The strained timbre to her voice reminded Cordero of someone in a panic. Was she frightened of him? If that was the case, he was glad he'd decided to stay. He wanted her to discover for herself that he was a gentleman, not a wolf in a cowboy's clothing.

"That's right. Your father persuaded me that I'd be doing you both a favor if I stuck around and helped you get acquainted with the horses." He gave her a harmless grin. "I'd feel pretty awful if I left and then you had a nasty fall or something."

Forget about the horses, Anne-Marie thought wildly. The only nasty tumble she was in danger of taking was for him. And that was something she wasn't about to let happen. Going back to her missionary work was all she wanted. And she intended to do just that as soon as her father was well enough to live on the plantation without her help.

Jules spoke up in an all-too-casual way. "Now that I think of it, Anne-Marie, I'd planned to take Cordero over to New Orleans tomorrow night for some blues music and dinner at Antoine's. Now that I'm stuck in this place, you'll have to take him." Jules tossed Cordero an innocent look. "If you've never visited the French Quarter, I think you'll find it a real treat."

Cordero had visited that colorful part of the city more than once. But with Anne-Marie as a guide, visiting Bourbon Street would be more than a treat. It would be a double dose of sensuality. Just the thought had his eyes sliding over her slim figure.

"Sounds nice. But Anne-Marie might have something else planned," Cordero said as diplomatically as he could.

Normally he'd pitch a fit if someone tried to manipulate him as this old man was doing. But he liked Jules. And a man would have to be crazy or half-dead not to want to spend time with a woman like Anne-Marie. It might be tricky to keep everything between them light and fun, he thought with a grain of concern, but he was damn well going to try.

Jules let out a mocking snort. "Don't worry about that. The last time Anne-Marie went out for entertainment, I still had black hair."

Anne-Marie gasped. "Father! Really! Cordero didn't come up here to get involved in our personal lives. And frankly—"

Jules interrupted her in a voice that had suddenly gone hoarse and weak. "I'm tired.

I need to get back in bed. You take Cordero on home and I'll talk to you about this tomorrow. "

Anne-Marie wanted to argue, but with her father looking so weary she bit her tongue and decided it would keep until later. After all, Cordero had already planned to stay at Cane's Landing for the coming week. Maybe one night of solitude, without her father around to entertain him, would make the man change his mind and head on back to Texas. No doubt Cordero had a bevy of girlfriends waiting there for him.

She sighed. "All right, Father. I'll call you tomorrow."

After she kissed his cheek and Cordero shook Jules's hand, they headed down the hospital corridor. When they were safely out of earshot, Anne-Marie whirled on Cordero.

"Why did you do that?" she asked through clenched teeth. "Why did you let him hire you like some common gigolo?"

His green eyes darkened to the color of a dangerous swamp and a muscle jumped in his clenched jaw. The anger on his face was a tangible thing and she swallowed hard as she eased a couple of steps back from him.

"Is that what you think?" He growled out the question. "That I hire myself out to pitiful spinsters who can't find themselves a man?"

Anne-Marie's nostrils flared as her temper shot straight to the top of her head. "Is that what you think I am? A pitiful spinster?" She heaved out a breath as she glanced frantically around to make sure no one was nearby. "Look, cowboy, I don't have to pay for a companion! Furthermore, I don't want one! Especially not the likes of you!"

He didn't say anything. Instead, he grabbed her by the arm and led her firmly toward the elevator. Once they stepped inside the cubicle, Anne-Marie prayed for someone, anyone, to join them, but the doors swished shut and the two of them were left alone.

Bracing herself for a volley of insults, she watched him push the button for the ground floor. But once the elevator stirred into motion, he surprised her by remaining stubbornly silent.

"What's the matter?" she finally asked in a sardonic voice. "Are you shocked that

I'm not falling in a worshipful heap at your feet?"

"No. I'm just waiting for the right moment to shut you up," he said with cool casualness. "And I think I've found it."

Jerking her head up to his, she opened her mouth to blast him with another retort. Instead, a silent *O* formed on her lips and she watched in shocked fascination as his head swooped toward hers.

Anne-Marie's dazed hesitation caused her to miss the chance to turn her head and gave him the perfect opportunity to plant his lips over hers.

She was so stunned by the intimate contact that she went stock-still. Her heart and lungs felt as though they'd stopped working as his mouth made a quick, thorough search of hers.

From somewhere inside her, heat rose up to scald the roots of her hair and scorch her cheeks. With each passing second, her knees grew weaker. She was about to grab onto the front of his shirt to keep from falling when he jerked up his head and gave her a cutting stare.

She said in a tight, low voice, "Whatever

was said between you and my father—this wasn't part of the deal!"

His black brows lifted to become two sardonic arches. "What makes you think you'd even be worth a deal?"

Her mind spun. She searched for the most ridiculing words she could find to hurl at him. But she didn't have to bother coming up with anything. The elevator doors opened and she marched out of the cubicle without him.

Behind her, she heard him chuckling and the cruel sound had her biting down on her swollen lip and blinking back tears. Damn the man. He wasn't worth crying over. No man was. Still, she couldn't stop one lone teardrop from rolling down her cheek.

She was in the foyer when, from behind, a pair of hands snaked around her waist. A gasp rushed past her lips as she spun around to face him.

"Let me go! Haven't you insulted me enough for one night?" Her words were pushed through clenched teeth as she tried to wriggle away from his grasp.

"Hold on a minute, Anne-Marie."

His voice was soft and threaded with regret. The sound stilled her and brought her eyes up to his.

He hurriedly tried to explain. "You've jumped to the wrong conclusions. Your father didn't hire me for anything. Jules is my friend. I only agreed to stay and help you with the horses because he asked me to. I agreed as a favor to him."

The grip he had on her waist eased to a warm clasp and Anne-Marie knew she was a fool for responding to it. But she'd never met a man like him before. One that could make her feel fury and passion all at the same time. It was scary.

"I'm sorry," she said after a moment. "I shouldn't have said any of those things to you. But this is all so—embarrassing. My father—it's obvious he's trying to manipulate us and I thought you'd agreed to go along with him."

Regret twisted his lips. "Forgive me, Anne-Marie. I shouldn't have reacted the way that I did. But I don't take too kindly to being called a gigolo."

Mortified all over again, Anne-Marie dropped her gaze to the floor. "Believe me, Cordero, I don't normally say that sort of thing to anyone. But Father has never put me in such an awkward situation before. I really don't know what he's thinking—I'm even beginning to worry that he's getting senile."

Cordero could have told her that there wasn't anything senile about Jules's mind. Calculating would be more like it, he thought wryly. But as far as he was concerned, the old man's manipulating was harmless. Even though that kiss he'd stolen in the elevator had jolted him right down to the heels of his boots, Cordero needed to make Anne-Marie see that she was taking this much too seriously.

"Look, Anne-Marie, we both need to take a deep breath and start over. There's really no need to make an issue out of this. Even if Jules is trying to maneuver us—we're adults, we can see through it. It won't hurt either of us to indulge a sick old man and pretend we're having a good time together these next few days." His hands slid gently down her forearms and the act was like brushing his fingers against a bird's wing. He'd never felt anything so soft, so fragile. "I have a feeling it would make him happy."

Anne-Marie didn't know what to make of his words. Confusion warred with the indignation she was already feeling toward this Texas cowboy who had kissed her as if he owned her. But perhaps he was right. She didn't want to put any undue stress on her father. And just because he was trying to throw her at Cordero didn't mean she had to fall into the cowboy's arms.

She drew in a troubled breath, then let it out. "I suppose you're right. But all that talk about taking you to Bourbon Street— that has nothing to do with you helping me with the horses. It was so obvious and humiliating."

Cordero suddenly grinned and she felt her stomach flutter as though she'd just swallowed a hummingbird.

"Actually, I thought your father's idea was a good one. I'd like for the two of us to make a trip to New Orleans. I'd planned on going anyway before I left for Texas and it would be far more enjoyable to have your company."

He was as smooth as water on a windless night, Anne-Marie thought, and just as enticing. If she ever really let her guard down around him, she'd be totally lost.

Trying not to dwell on that danger, she said, "We'll see. Right now we'd better go home. Darcella is waiting to serve supper."

He silently complied by taking her arm and leading her out of the double doors. By now darkness had fallen and Anne-Marie felt the confines of the car even more with only the dim lights from the dashboard illuminating the small space between them.

She tried to close her eyes and pretend his long lean body wasn't there beside her, but his presence was too strong to ignore. The scent of him drifted to her, reminding her of wide-open ranges, sagebrush and wild mustangs. It was a scent that called to her senses and all she could think about was the feel of his lips upon hers, the warm touch of his fingers on her arm.

The practical part of her wished that he'd never kissed her, but the woman in her was still swooning, still wondering what it would be like if he were to take her into his arms and really kiss her with desire. It was indecent of her to think such things. She didn't even know the man. Only a few hours had passed since she'd first laid eyes on him. Yet something about him had stirred up ashes in her that she'd believed were stone-cold. She had to find her will to resist.

"I'm not a doctor, but I thought your father looked pretty good."

Cordero's comment jerked Anne-Marie out of her erotic thoughts. "Yes, I thought so, too. His doctor says he doesn't think this little flare-up is anything to be concerned about. I think he's just taking extra precautions with my father's health."

What would she think, he wondered, if she knew Jules had purposely put himself in the hospital so it would force her to play hostess to Cordero? She'd really think the man had gone senile. But Cordero had no intention of giving away his friend's secret. It would be no gain to any of them and only cause worse feelings all around. "I'm glad," he said. "Your father is a great guy. He's always laughing and full of jokes."

His remark surprised her. Most young men didn't have time or patience when it came to dealing with the older generation. Some of them only feigned respect for their elders. Like Ian, she thought bitterly. He couldn't have cared less about her father. And she'd been stupid for believing that he'd loved Jules any more than he'd loved her. The guy had only cared about two things. Himself and money.

"Father has always been full of life. Even after Mama died he managed to hold himself together and find joy in other things. I realize he wants me to be more fun-loving, like him. But I'm just not made that way."

Cordero had known for a long time that Jules was a widower. He'd not thought much about that until he'd met Anne-Marie. She was young. Her mother couldn't have been very old when she'd passed away. And the fact that the two of them had prematurely lost their mothers connected him to her in a way he'd never expected.

"How long has your mother been gone?" he asked.

"Sixteen years. I was ten at the time. She died quite suddenly from an aneurysm. For a long time after that Father couldn't bear to look at the horses. You see, they belonged to Mama. She rode all the time."

Cordero heard something more than sadness in her voice; a tinge of bitterness edged her words. It made him wonder exactly what sort of relationship she'd had with her mother. Or maybe she was angry with God for taking away her parent? Maybe losing her mother had more to do with her not entering a convent than her broken affair? He could only guess.

"And now it's just you and your father?" he asked quietly. "You don't have any siblings?"

Anne-Marie shook her head. "No. I was an only child and Father was never interested in remarrying."

"Neither is mine."

He could feel her blue eyes on his face and he darted another glance at her.

"Your mother is dead, too?" she asked with surprise.

Cordero nodded. "Seven years ago. Complications from diabetes. She was only fifty-six."

"Oh. Then you know how it feels to have a parent gone."

His throat grew so tight that for a moment all he could do was manage a nod. He'd been very close to his mother, far closer than his older brother, Matt, or his

sister, Lucita. Which seemed strange whenever he thought about it. He was a replica
of his father, who had a magic hand with a
horse and had taught Cordero everything
he knew about raising the animals. Cordero was also like Mingo in the fact that he
loved a pretty woman's company and considered life something to be enjoyed rather
than endured. He loved and respected his
father, who was thankfully alive and well
today. But his mother still lived like the
warm glow of a candle in his heart. And
after seven years without her, he missed her.
Really missed her.

"Yeah. It's tough," he murmured. "Damn
tough."

He could feel her regarding him with
a thoughtful eye, but she didn't say more
about his mother. Cordero was glad. He
didn't want to dwell on that part of his past.

Reaching across the seat, he folded his
hand around hers. "Let's not think about
such sad things. I want to enjoy these next
few days and I hope you'll enjoy them with
me."

His fingers were warm, the skin hardened
with calluses. She tried not to think how

they would feel sliding across her naked skin or cupping her breasts, but the images wouldn't budge from her mind. Her whole body flushed with heat as she swallowed and turned her head toward the passenger window.

"I'm not a fun sort of woman, Cordero. I'm afraid you're going to end up being very bored during your stay at Cane's Landing."

His fingers tightened on hers. "Maybe I can teach you how to have a little fun."

Anne-Marie wasn't about to ask him what sort of fun he had in mind. The man was already putting sinful thoughts in her head. She didn't need any more added to them. And as for having fun, she wasn't at all sure she'd ever known how to enjoy herself as other young women seemed to do. From the time of her mother's death, she'd viewed life as a serious journey. Even her relationship with Ian had been slowly and carefully entered into, one step at a time.

She still hadn't replied to his suggestive words when the footlights illuminating the turnoff to Cane's Landing came into view. Glad for any reason to ease her hand from beneath his, she motioned toward the entrance leading off the left side of the black-top road. "There's our turnoff."

The drive up the tree-lined lane to the house took less than two minutes. Once they were out of the car, Cordero offered her his arm for the walk through the dark shadows between the garage and the house. Anne-Marie realized that touching him, for any reason, was not something she should do. But he was being a gentleman and it wasn't his fault that her senses went haywire around him, so she curled her arm through his and rested her hand on his strong forearm.

As they passed Cordero's truck, Anne-Marie suggested that it might be a good time to get his bags. After he pulled out two leather duffel bags, he offered her his arm again and they made their way into the house.

Darcella met them in the front room. The cook was a tall, big-boned woman with graying brown hair that was cut in a pixie style that framed her round face. Her wide smile seemed to deepen as she spotted Anne-Marie's arm looped through

Cordero's. Anne-Marie knew that Darcella had been initially shocked when she'd first met the Texas rancher. Both women had expected Jules's friend to be much closer to his age. That assumption couldn't have been more off base.

"How was Mr. Jules?" the cook asked. "Feeling better?"

Anne-Marie sighed as she slipped her arm from Cordero's and moved away from his side. "He seemed full of life," she told the woman. "In fact, I think he looked better than he has in months."

"Oh. That's good. Real good. Maybe he'll get to come home soon."

"We're all hoping that, Darcella." Anne-Marie walked across the room and placed her handbag on a small table.

Behind her, Darcella said, "Well, I've left a tray of drinks out on the back porch. I thought you two would like to unwind before I serve supper."

Walking back to the center of the room, Anne-Marie glanced from Darcella to Cordero then back again. She wanted to tell the cook that there was no need to make a big deal out of this supper. She didn't want Cordero to get the impression that she was going out of her way to entertain him. But if she urged Darcella to leave, it would only look as if she wanted to be alone with the man.

Stifling a groan, she turned to Cordero and tried to smile. "Darcella has gone to a lot of trouble to make mint juleps for us tonight."

"Sounds great." He looked at the cook and gave her a conspiring wink. "Darcella, if you're not a married woman, you need to come to the Sandbur sometime and meet our cook. Juan's a little older than you but he's single and he loves to dance. He makes a mean margarita, too."

Darcella giggled in a way that Anne-Marie had never heard before.

"I might just do that some time, Mr. Sanchez. Especially if Anne-Marie would come with me."

Cordero turned a suggestive look to Anne-Marie, who quickly cleared her throat and changed the subject completely.

"Come on," she invited. "I'll show you

to your room. After you've had a chance to freshen up, we'll go to the porch for those drinks."

She started toward a long, curving staircase and Cordero picked up his bags and followed. As he climbed one step behind her, he allowed his gaze to swing around the massive room below. The large area was lit with only two small lamps, but even in the semidarkness he could see the rich antique furniture typical of the antebellum period. The walls were covered with heavy paper printed with trailing vines and some sort of maroon flower. The balustrade along the staircase and the upstairs landing was made of polished cypress and smelled faintly of lemon wax. The only sound to be heard was the faint ticking of a tall, grandfather clock.

This afternoon, when Anne-Marie had shown him into the parlor, he'd gotten the feeling that he'd stepped back in time. Now, as he followed her up through the dark quietness, that same sensation hit him again.

Once they reached the landing, she walked to the end and pushed open a door on her right. "I hope you'll find the room agreeable. Verbena, our maid, made sure there were fresh towels and washcloths in the bath." She pointed to a door in the far corner of the room. "But if you need anything else, just let me know."

The bed was an enormous oak four-poster with a dark green duvet. On the outer wall, several feet away, were three tall windows covered with sheer beige curtains. Beyond the windowpanes, he could barely discern the shape of huge tree limbs, but nothing else.

"You can store your things here in the dresser, if you like." She opened one of the top drawers. "You won't disturb anything. This is just a guest room. And it's been ages since anyone has visited."

Cordero got the feeling that time here on the plantation moved at glacial speed so it would be hard to interpret what she meant by ages. He couldn't help but wonder if her ex-lover had stayed here, perhaps even in this room. He hated to think so. For some unexplainable reason he didn't want to be connected to the guy in any way.

"Thanks, Anne-Marie. I'm sure everything will be fine."

He placed his duffel bag on the end of the bed and wondered why he felt so awkward and out of place in this opulent bedroom. He was not a poor man. In fact, the Sandbur was known all over South Texas. He was used to fairly lavish surroundings and servants at his beck and call. But his home in Texas was laid-back. It invited a man to kick off his boots and prop his feet on the furniture. This place was a little stiff for his liking. Or was it the kiss he'd planted on Anne-Marie's lips that was really bothering him? He couldn't forget it. Even now, he wanted to pull her into his arms and kiss her until they both ended up on the four-poster behind him. He was a man who'd always liked women, but he'd never encountered one that had taken such a hold on him in a matter of hours.

Something of what Cordero was feeling must have shown on his face because she suddenly folded her hands together and began to inch backward toward the door.

"Good," she said. "I'll meet you at the bottom of the landing in five minutes."

His gaze settled on her rose-pink lips. "Yeah. Five minutes. See you then."

With a stilted nod, she hurried out of the room. Once she'd closed the door behind her, Cordero wiped a hand over his face and wondered what in hell he'd gotten himself into.

Chapter Three

When Anne-Marie came down from her bedroom a few minutes later, Cordero was waiting for her at the bottom of the staircase. The white-and-blue windowpane shirt he'd been wearing had been exchanged for a dark red cotton. The rich color only intensified the deep brown of his skin and made his white teeth appear that much whiter. He didn't bother to hide the appreciation in his eyes as she descended the stairs, but Anne-Marie tried her best not to dwell on it as she joined him on the polished parquet.

"Since I don't know which way to go, you'd better lead me," he murmured.

Anne-Marie didn't resist his warm hand as it wrapped around hers, but as she led him through the house, she promised herself that once their houseguest had gone back to Texas, her father was going to get a piece of her mind. Jules had made it quite clear for some time now that he wanted her to get out of the house and date young men, to put some excitement in her life, but she'd never dreamed he would take matters into his own hands and practically thrust her into Cordero Sanchez's arms. Jules needed to learn once and for all that she was going to lead her own life and it wasn't going to have a man in it.

The back porch ran the total width of the house and was enclosed with screen to keep the ever-present mosquitoes at bay. Comfortable lawn furniture was scattered from one end of the space to the other, along with many potted plants, some of which were covered with vivid blooms.

A wicker settee and armchairs padded with bright yellow cushions sat at the far end of the porch and it was here that Darcella had left the tray of drinks.

Anne-Marie extricated her hand from Cordero's and took a seat on the settee. To her dismay, he dropped his long frame down next to her.

"This is nice," he said. "Quiet. But nice."

Leaning forward, she picked up two squatty tumblers and handed one to him. His fingers brushed against hers as he took the cool, sweaty glass and for one brief moment she wished he would reach over and take her hand again. Touching him thrilled her and reminded her that she was still a flesh-and-blood woman. Something she'd been desperately trying to forget since her downfall at Ian's hands.

"Your home on the ranch isn't quiet?" she asked.

He laughed and the deep gravelly sound sent shivers of pleasure rushing over her skin while inside her the need to slide away from his side fought wildly with the urge to wiggle closer.

"Uh, not too often. My brother, Matt, and his family live in the same house. They have a teenage daughter and a baby on the way. And Dad lives with us, too. Things can get rowdy when all of us are home. But the house is big and we wouldn't know any other way, except being together."

Being together. Those two words reminded her of happier times. When her mother had still been alive and the three of them had been a family. Now she clung to her father, afraid that soon she would lose him, too. It wasn't the way a young woman like her was supposed to be living. Except for Jules, and two cousins in Thibodaux, she was alone. And somehow being here with Cordero and listening to him speak of his family only reminded her of that fact even more.

"Your family is important to you. I can tell," she said.

Grooves of amusement bracketed his lips. "You sound like that surprises you."

A faint blush of heat filtered into her cheeks. "Fun-loving guys like you don't usually put importance on much of anything. Except the next party. The next girl."

"Ouch. Why didn't you just pinch me?" he asked drily, then shook his head. "I hate to tell you this, Anne-Marie, but you don't know me. You're trying to draw a picture without really understanding the subject."

Maybe she wasn't being fair in her assessment, she thought. But it didn't matter. She couldn't let herself really get to know him. He lived in a different world and soon he would be going back to it. Something told her that a momentary fling with this man would be even more devastating to her heart than Ian's drawn-out deception.

"You're right. I don't know you well enough to make those sorts of comments." She cautiously sipped her julep, then glanced at him over the rim of her glass. "How do you like your drink?"

He chuckled. "It's good, but I can already feel a wallop. What did Darcella put in these things anyway?"

She smiled. "I think she made them out of vodka and she uses a heavy hand. I should have warned you."

"For a man who's only used to one or two beers at a time, I think one of these things is all I can handle."

Her glance turned a bit teasing. "What about those mean margaritas that your cook at the Sandbur makes?"

Another chuckle rolled out of him. "Oh. We only have those on special occasions. Like birthdays, weddings, anniversaries." His eyes softened as they roamed over her face. "But if you decide to come to the ranch, I'm sure we'd all view it as a special occasion."

The touch of his gaze was almost as heady as the trail of his fingers over hers. His eyes were a tricky color to label. They held too many brown flecks to call them green and too much green to call them brown. Altogether they were like green leaves dappled with golden sunshine and the thick veil of black lashes surrounding them only intensified their vivid color.

Feeling a flutter in her stomach that had nothing to do with the strong julep, she placed her glass back on the tray and rose to her feet.

"I'm getting very hungry. If you're finished with that, let's go in and eat," she suggested.

Cordero could have argued. For him it was a slice of heaven to be out here alone with her. Especially with the strong, sweet drink warming his already heated blood and the frogs and locusts singing a night-time symphony. But she seemed eager to leave the porch and he didn't want to irk her again. Not after he'd witnessed a glimpse of her temper at the hospital. The idea of spending the next few days around a stirred-up hornet, even a beautiful one, wasn't exactly his idea of fun.

Inside the house, Anne-Marie directed him to the dining room, a large square space with tall ceilings and two chandeliers hanging over a long, oak table. But the tiny slabs of crystal weren't shedding any light from overhead. Instead, six candles spaced at intervals in the middle of the table shed a soft yellow glow over the settings of delicate china.

Beside him, he heard Anne-Marie gasp. "What in the world is Darcella thinking? We never eat by candlelight! I'll turn on the lights."

She turned to walk over to the light switch on the wall, but Cordero caught her by the wrist. "Don't do that," he urged. "She's gone to a lot of trouble. And I think it's nice."

Hell, what was *he* thinking? He wasn't a man who made a habit of having romantic candlelit dinners with a woman. He did well to take her to an eating place where the forks were real stainless steel instead of plastic. But something about Cane's Landing and the woman standing at his side made him want to experience things he'd never dreamed of before. The whole notion was damned unsettling.

He watched her lips compress with disapproval and then she shrugged as though it was nothing to make an issue over. "All right. But just so you know, I didn't ask for this."

"I didn't think for one minute that you had," he said wryly.

She threw him a look that was mostly confused and he felt compelled to add, "You don't seem the type."

Pulling her wrist from his grasp, she asked a bit warily, "What type is that?"

"The type to purposely set out to seduce a man."

"Oh."

If she was insulted by his comment she deftly covered her feelings as she walked over to the table and waited for him to help her into one of the high-backed chairs.

By the time Cordero had taken his seat at the end of the table, Darcella arrived with their first dish. As she placed the small bowls of spicy shrimp gumbo in front of them, he complimented the woman on the beautiful table and the mint juleps.

Darcella gave Cordero a wide, toothy grin. "Thank you, Cordero." She turned a pointed look on Anne-Marie. "I'm glad someone around here appreciates me."

After the cook left the room, Anne-Marie tilted her face toward the ceiling and wearily shook her head. "Cordero, you must be thinking Father and Darcella are manipulators of the worst kind." She turned a helpless look on him, then gestured toward the lighted candles. "Just, please, overlook all this."

Overlook it? He couldn't. Being with her like this was nigh irresistible and he didn't care who was doing the manipulating as long as he was sitting across from her watching the candlelight flicker across her lovely face.

With a placating smile, he said, "You're worrying too much about nothing, Anne-Marie. Let's just enjoy our supper."

They'd hardly finished the first course when Darcella returned with a platter of fried catfish, hush puppies and pan-fried potatoes.

"Be sure and save room for dessert," she warned as she left the dining room.

"Dessert? Is she kidding?" Cordero asked.

Anne-Marie shook her head. "No. She's made one of her famous chocolate cakes. And if you like sweets, you don't want to miss it." She glanced at him as she placed a small helping of fish on her plate. "It's no wonder Father has heart trouble. He's enjoyed Darcella's cooking for many years and her menus aren't exactly low in cholesterol."

Cordero grunted with amusement. "That's why it tastes so good."

"Well, to be fair, Darcella does try to cook healthy things for Father. But most of those things end up being thrown in the trash. He says food is one of man's pleasures in life and he doesn't intend to miss out."

Cordero thrust his glass of iced tea toward her in a cheeky salute. "I'll say amen to that."

She rolled her eyes, but the faint upward

curve to her lips said that she understood all
about a man's weakness for physical pleasures. The idea teased his thoughts with all
sorts of erotic images and for the remainder
of the meal he found he couldn't keep his
eyes off her. Candlelight bathed her face and
throat and turned her skin to golden satin.
The glow of the tiny flames sparked her
red hair with flickering highlights and more
than once he had to fight the urge to reach
across the corner of the table and mesh his
fingers in the long burnished strands lying
against her breast.

Two days ago he'd been attending his
cousin Nicci's wedding at the Sandbur. Hundreds of people had swarmed the ranch for
the reception that had been held outside in
the shaded backyard of the Saddler house.
Eating and drinking, dancing and foot-
stomping laughter had taken place until the
wee hours of the morning. There had been
plenty of young, beautiful women among
the guests and most of them hadn't been shy
about wanting Cordero's attention. But now,
as he looked at Anne-Marie, he realized that
none of them had affected him as much as
she was affecting him now. And what shook

him the most was that she wasn't even trying to tempt him.

What would happen to him, he wondered wildly, if he was able to seduce her? Would he be able to go back to Texas and forget her? Or would making love to her burn him like one of Matt's hot branding irons burned cowhide?

At some point in his tangled thoughts, Cordero realized Anne-Marie's lips were moving, but he hadn't heard a word she'd said.

"Uh, sorry, Anne-Marie. You were saying something?"

With slow, graceful movements, she pulled a linen napkin from her lap and placed it next to her plate. "I was saying that if you've finished eating, you might like to take a walk in the backyard garden. It's still too early for bed and it's pleasant out there at this time of night."

Hoping the grin on his face wasn't as wolfish as it felt, Cordero hurriedly left his chair and helped her to her feet.

As they left the dining room, he took the opportunity to slip his arm around her back. The moment he touched her, he could feel her body tense, but after they took a few steps she seemed to relax and accept the weight of his hand resting in the curve of her waist.

In a matter of moments they were on the porch where they'd left the juleps. There, a screen door led down several wooden steps and onto a neat trail covered with washed river gravel.

Anne-Marie inclined her head toward an archway tangled with moon blossom vines. "Through there," she said. "The footlights are enough light."

By now the sun had been down for a couple of hours and the temperature was cooling to a bearable level. The faint breeze stirring the oak leaves above their heads helped ward off the occasional mosquito.

Cordero felt a strange sense of peace as he looked around at the carefully groomed rosebushes and smelled the pungent scent of jasmine. "I noticed this part of the backyard when we hauled the horses down to the stables," he said to Anne-Marie. "I thought it looked like something in an Old Spanish courtyard or a private garden behind a sanctuary."

"I suppose it does. My mother built this garden shortly after she married Father. She was a deeply religious person and I think she liked to use this as a quiet place to pray."

"Did she work as a missionary, too?" Cordero asked as they strolled along the winding trail.

"No. She was a high school music teacher. But she did lots of church work."

"Is she the reason you thought about entering a convent?" Even as he asked the question, Cordero couldn't imagine this warm, vibrant woman next to him making a vow of chastity. One look at her was enough to tell him she was meant to love a man and have his children.

Her chin dropped and she kept her eyes on the ground as they continued deeper into the garden. "Maybe. I think I always viewed her as an angel. She seemed so perfect. And I wanted to be like her."

Cordero smiled faintly. "That's because she was your mother. You were viewing her through very young eyes."

Her gaze slipped up to his shadowed face. "She had friends from all over Assumption and St. James parishes and she had a special way of taking care of others—people who were sick or emotionally needy. As I grew older I thought becoming a sister would be the best way to give of myself—like she did. But that wasn't meant to be. I learned I—well, I'm not worthy."

Cordero couldn't believe she'd said such a thing about herself. He wanted to press her about the comment, but she suddenly changed the subject completely. "Do you know anything about sugarcane?"

He laughed. "The only thing I know is that I like desserts and I like molasses poured over a hot biscuit."

A smile tugged at her lips. "Maybe I could show you some of the fields tomorrow and give you a little lesson," she suggested. "If you'd like, that is."

He'd made a big mistake, Cordero thought, as he gazed down at her beautiful face. He should never have agreed to stay here alone with her, even for a few days. One evening with this woman was turning him into a complete fool. He felt like a teenager, raging hormones were directing his brain. What would he be like after spending a few days with her?

Don't worry about it, Cordero, once you're back in Texas nothing about Anne-Marie Duveuil will matter. You've been temporarily enchanted with a woman before. This one is no different.

The little voice in his head was enough to momentarily push the nagging question out of Cordero's mind and his fingers tightened on the side of her waist.

"I'd like it a lot," he murmured, then remarked, "Your home here is really something. Has it always been in your family?"

She nodded. "The Duveuils have always been here. Our family tree goes back to some of the first Acadians who settled this area. My ancestors were part of the French Acadians that had to flee Canada in 1755. They came down here to Louisiana when it was still just a Spanish colony. I'm sure at that time most of my distant relatives were trappers. But down through the years the Duveuils began to farm and we've raised sugarcane here in the river bottoms for nearly two hundred years."

Anne-Marie was relieved to see the wrought-iron bench come into view. Maybe if they sat down, he'd be forced to take his hand away and she could put some distance between them. Otherwise, with his fingers dipping into her flesh, she could scarcely think about anything except the excitement that was rushing through her, making her heart beat way too fast.

"Let's sit," she suggested and, pulling away from his hold on her, she walked to the bench and took a seat at one end.

In front of her, slightly to the left, was an old concrete fountain built in the image of an angel. Most of the fountain was covered with moss and algae, making a major portion of the figure a muted green color. Water trickled from a large jug cradled in the cherub's hands and splashed like musical notes into the pool surrounding her feet. Normally the sound of the cascading water soothed Anne-Marie, but tonight, with Cordero easing down on the seat next to her, she could hardly hear it for her pulse pounding in her ears.

"I feel like a bull in a china shop," he said wryly, as he took in the delicate white roses encircling the fountain. "Maybe we should go back to the porch."

Anne-Marie's gaze settled on his brown

cowboy boots. The toes were slightly rounded, the heels slanted and high. She could easily picture him in spurs and chaps, cracking a whip at a charging bull. "Why? Don't you like it out here?"

"It's beautiful. The roses look like something out of a gardening magazine. But it's—" He glanced around as though he expected to find someone standing in the shadows. "I get the feeling someone is here—watching us. I feel like I'm intruding."

Anne-Marie wondered what it meant that he felt the presence, too. No one else had. Not even Jules.

"I think it's Mama's spirit. I guess that's why I love this garden so much." She let out a wistful sigh, then glanced at him. "Tell me about your ranch. What does it look like?"

He leaned back in the seat and crossed his boots at the ankles. Anne-Marie was glad to see the mention of a spirit hadn't spooked him or made him laugh at her as Ian used to.

"The Sandbur is a big property. It covers several thousands of acres. In the main ranch yard, there are lots of corrals and fences and barns. We employ cowboys to take care of the cattle and the horses."

"Does all your family live on the ranch? In one house?"

With a fond smile curving his lips, he picked up her hand and gently rubbed his thumb against the soft skin of her palm. Anne-Marie swallowed as her heart kicked into an even higher gear. She didn't know why the memory of that kiss he'd planted on her in the elevator was still rattling around in her head like a dangerous bullet. She should have forgotten the whole thing. Instead, those moments seemed to be growing more and more vivid in her mind.

"Most of my family lives on the ranch," he said. "But not in the same house. There are two main houses on the Sandbur. The Sanchez house and the Saddler house, which belongs to my Aunt Geraldine. My cousin Lex lives with her. He's in charge of sales and marketing."

"Is he married?"

Her question brought a loud guffaw from him. "Not on your life! Lex is like me. He enjoys his freedom too much to let a woman tie him down. He's about to turn thirty-five and he hasn't been married yet. I doubt he'll ever walk down the aisle."

So Cordero viewed marriage as something to avoid. The confession didn't surprise her. He had that look about him. She'd noticed it when she'd first seen him. He was like a wild mustang that valued freedom more than a bucket of grain and a pat on the head. Being bridled wasn't his style and she'd be very smart to keep remembering that.

"Does Lex have siblings?"

"Two sisters. Nicci just got married a couple of days ago. She's a doctor and married a doctor. And then there's Mercedes. She's in the air force. I think her stint is about up. But you can never tell about Mercedes, she just might reenlist."

The eagerness to know more about this man unwittingly caused her to turn toward him. Her knees bumped into his, but she didn't jerk them away. Even though it shouldn't matter, she didn't want him thinking she was that prim and proper spinster who couldn't find herself a man.

"What about your immediate family?

You mentioned a brother. Is he the only sibling you have?"

"No. I also have a sister. Lucita lives in Corpus Christi and teaches school there. She's divorced and has a ten-year-old son. We're trying to get her to come back to the Sandbur to live, but so far we haven't been able to persuade her. As for Matt, he remarried a little more than a year ago after being a widower for seven years. He's the general manager of the ranch and oversees the cattle production."

"Sounds like a busy man," Anne-Marie mused aloud.

Cordero nodded. "He used to work night and day. In fact, his whole life was work. But his new wife changed all of that. Now he makes sure he takes time out for her and their daughter."

Anne-Marie sighed wistfully as she pictured his big family. No doubt they had gatherings during holidays and special occasions. If one needed help there would always be another to lean on. How would it feel to be sheltered in such a warm nest?

"I've always believed I would be a different person if I'd had a brother or sister to share things with. But unfortunately that never happened. After Mama gave birth to me, she wasn't physically able to bear more children."

He must have picked up on the sad note in her voice because his fingers wrapped around hers and squeezed. Anne-Marie was becoming addicted to the strength of his hand, the security it lent her. Which was crazy. She hardly knew this man. Yet she was drawn to him in ways that shook her deeply.

"I'm sorry," he said. "And I say that because I know how lost I'd be without my brother and sister, my cousins. We're braided together like a piece of lariat. If one of us hurts, the rest do, too."

Her expression turned reflective as it drifted over to the fountain. "Yes. I got the feeling it would be that way with your family. Just hearing about them is…nice."

She could feel his gaze wandering over her face like a lover's meandering hand. The lure of it pulled her eyes around to his face and the chiseled curve of his lips. Desire, wild and sweet, rushed through her veins and heated her cheeks.

"I don't guess your parents considered adopting a brother or sister for you?" he asked.

Dropping her eyes from the tempting sight of him, Anne-Marie shook her head. "Father was against it. I really don't know why, except that he had to share Mama with me, and so many others, who often called on Fiona for help of some kind or another. I think he just didn't want her attention taken away from him any more than it already was."

"Hmm. Well, do you have any other relatives around?"

She shrugged one shoulder. "I have a few older aunts and uncles on my mother's side. But they and their families are scattered across the South. I don't see them very often. My cousins, Audra and Emmett, are the only ones I stay in touch with. They're Duveuils and live in Thibodaux. Their father, Neville, and Jules were brothers. But he passed away a few years ago and their mother married and left the area."

"You implied that this place has always been a family operation. Did Neville ever have anything to do with Cane's Landing?"

"Years ago he did. But then he sold his part of the place to my father. Now it belongs solely to Jules. Cane's Landing will eventually go to me whenever he's gone."

Cordero's fingers unwrapped themselves from hers to slowly slide up her forearm. Anne-Marie tried not to shiver as goose bumps erupted across her skin.

"This is a big place for one little woman," he remarked. "Do you plan on keeping it?"

Something in the air between them was sizzling, warning her to get up and away before she got burned. But her brain refused to send a signal to her legs.

"I'd never sell Cane's Landing. There are plenty of employees to take care of the grounds and the crops."

Leaning closer, his voice lowered. "I don't mean that, Anne-Marie. Living here alone would be—well, it just wouldn't be the right thing for a woman like you."

Her tongue peeped out to slide moisture against her top lip. "And you know what the right thing for me would be?"

Suddenly she realized his hand had made its way to her shoulder and now his fingers were twining through her hair. She could feel her breaths growing shorter and shorter while her eyelids insisted on drifting downward.

"Not exactly," he said in a low voice. "I just know that you were meant to have a man in your life."

She shouldn't be feeling this drunk, Anne-Marie thought. She'd only taken a few tiny sips of mint julep. She drew in a deep breath in hopes of clearing her foggy senses. "You're not thinking you're that man, are you?"

His soft chuckle was warm and sexy and whispered against her cheeks like a tempting breeze on a hot night.

"I don't see any other man around here at the moment."

Chapter Four

Knowing she was about to drown and that this was the last chance to save herself, Anne-Marie started to rise from the bench. But his hands quickly caught her forearms and tugged her even closer to the front of his body.

Her heart beating in her throat, she protested, "Cordero, you're only going to be here for a few days. That—"

He interrupted by murmuring, "That means we need to make the most of our time together."

His voice was so sultry and sensual she

felt as though he'd wrapped her in a velvet cloak. The soft warmth was melting her bones.

A tiny, helpless moan sounded in her throat as she watched his head descend toward hers. But even that pitiful objection came to an abrupt end as his lips captured hers in one swift swoop.

The intimate contact momentarily robbed her of breath and then all she could think was that this was nothing like the kiss he'd given her in the elevator. His lips were making a slow, seductive foray over hers. Searching and teasing, spreading a sensation of liquid heat throughout her body. This kiss was shouting that he wanted her and she had no choice but to answer that she wanted him just as much.

His hands traveled over her shoulders and down her back until they met at her waist, where they pressed her even closer. The movement caused her lower body to twist completely off the bench and then somehow she found herself tugged onto his lap, her head cradled against his strong shoulder.

Somewhere around them, she heard the frogs and insects singing in glorious unison.

A leaf fluttered and the water poured from the angel's jug tinkled a hypnotic melody. But the sounds were muted by the roaring heartbeats in her ears.

Desire and fear wrapped themselves together and thudded inside her like a war drum. Urging her to make love to him. Urging her to pull away.

Before her mind and her body could come to agreement, Cordero finally lifted his mouth from hers and smiled.

"See what I mean?" he whispered. "Can you think of a nicer way to spend the next few days?"

The provocative tone of his words was like turning on a warning siren. It jolted Anne-Marie out of her romantic stupor and she bolted from his lap.

With her gaze fastened warily on his face, she backed away from him and the bench until her hips were resting against the rim of the fountain. "You're not here for this— that—me!"

In the blink of an eye he was standing next to her, his big hands cupping the sides of her face. She breathed in the scent of him and felt her legs tremble.

"That's not what your lips told me a few moments ago," he countered. "That's not what they're going to tell me now, either."

She'd not expected him to kiss her again and though her body was begging her to fall into his arms, common sense sent her running to another part of the garden where the air was thick with the scent of honeysuckle and the shadows were deep and dark. She was breathing hard, her fingertips rubbing back and forth across her swollen lips when he quietly slipped up behind her. As his hands came down on her shoulders she tried not to groan with longing.

"I'm sorry, Anne-Marie," he said gently. "I didn't mean to push myself on you."

Swallowing the tightness in her throat, she turned to face him. "No. Don't apologize. I'm the one who should be doing that. You weren't behaving out of character. I was. I should never have kissed you that way. I was leading you on—and that was wrong of me."

"It didn't feel wrong."

She sighed. "Well, it was. I have no intention of ever getting involved with another man. Even for a few brief days. Even with you."

His expression sober, his hands momentarily tightened on her shoulders. "That sounds...very lonely, Anne-Marie."

A strange sort of sadness swept through her, but she pushed it away. Pleasure had nearly ruined her once; she was determined never to take that path again.

"There are other things in life besides romance and marriage. Once Father's health is better I intend to return to my missionary work. That's the thing in life that brings me solace. That's all I want."

What about joy and happiness? Didn't that fit into her life, too? Cordero wanted to ask her. But he kept the questions to himself. Frankly, he was in no shape to spar with the woman. The kiss he'd just shared with her had been something far beyond a meeting of lips. Though he didn't want to admit it to himself, he'd never experienced anything like it. Everything inside him was still shaking and he felt drunk with the desire to hold her again.

The best thing he could do now was get the hell out of here. Two more days and that would be it, Cordero promised himself. By Thursday he was heading back to Texas. Before this redheaded angel had him thinking he wanted to be caught for a lifetime.

"Well, maybe we'd better go in," he suddenly suggested. "It's been a long day."

She glanced at his face. "You're angry at me. I can tell by the frown on your face."

His frown had nothing to do with her and everything to do with the realization that his weakness for women was someday going to get him into trouble. Maybe it already had.

He smiled to soften his words. "I'm not the least bit angry, Anne-Marie. A man has to try. I lost and that's that." He reached for her hand and urged her back onto the graveled path. "Come on. I feel a need for another one of Darcella's mint juleps."

On the porch, she waited by the door while he poured himself a drink from the pitcher they'd left behind. Taking it with him, he entered the house with her and they climbed the stairs together.

Both of them were silent until they reached the landing. Then Anne-Marie offered him an awkward good-night, before she fled to her bedroom.

Cordero went into his own room and shut the door behind him. He gulped the vodka down in three long swigs and was glad when a buzz almost immediately hit his brain. He didn't want to think tonight. He didn't want to remember the feeling of Anne-Marie in his arms.

Jerking his cell phone out of his pocket, he sank onto the edge of the bed and quickly dialed the Sanchez house.

His niece, Gracia, answered the phone on the third ring.

"Gracia, it's Cordero. Is your daddy around?"

"Hi, Uncle Cordero! We've all been wondering about you! Daddy said you must be in a beer joint or a jail cell. Otherwise, we would have heard from you before now."

With a wry grimace, Cordero said, "Well, I'm not in either. So tell Matt to get himself to the phone."

"Okay. Hang on a sec. Him and Mom are out on the patio."

Love had definitely changed his older brother for the better, Cordero thought. Matt was always laughing and smiling now. He didn't drive himself into the ground. Instead, he quit before dark and went home to enjoy his family. But then Matt had always been a family man. Cordero wouldn't know what to do with a wife or child. And he didn't want to learn—especially how it felt to lose one.

"Cordero? Where the hell are you?"

Matt's voice boomed in his ear and for a second he forgot that he was still in Louisiana in a plantation house that had seen centuries of families come and go.

He stifled a sigh. "I'm in Louisiana. I got here earlier this afternoon."

"Did you make it okay? Any trouble with the truck? The horses?"

"No. Everything went great."

"That's good. Did Jules like the horses?"

Cordero closed his eyes and rubbed the burning lids with his fingertips. "He hasn't seen them yet. He's in the hospital."

"Hospital! What happened?"

Nothing, Cordero wanted to bark at him. The old man looked as fit as a fiddle. But he couldn't explain to Matt that Jules Duveuil was playing a part for his daughter's benefit. The whole thing was too bizarre to explain.

"A little trouble with his heart. He's having tests run. But I'm sure he's going to be okay."

"You've seen him?"

"Yes. His daughter went with me to the hospital."

"Grown daughter?"

Normally the note of suspicion in Matt's voice would have had him laughing, but at the moment Cordero couldn't summon up an ounce of amusement.

"That's right. Actually the horses are for her."

"Oh. Well, I hope she was pleased with them. Did you assure her that the Sandbur will buy them back if she doesn't like the way they perform?"

Cordero frowned. "Since when did you start questioning me about my job?" he asked shortly. "You take care of the cattle and let me handle the horses. Okay?"

There was a long pause, then Matt said in a low, rough voice, "What the hell is the matter with you?"

Feeling ashamed of his sudden outburst, Cordero sighed. "Sorry, Matt. I didn't mean that. I'm just dog-tired. And this place is getting to me."

"What place? You haven't said where you are? Are you already on your way back home?"

Dropping his hand from his eyes, he glanced around the comfortably furnished room. "No. I'm at Cane's Landing. I'm staying here for the rest of the week just as I'd planned."

"I don't understand. With Jules in the hospital you two can't do much visiting," Matt said.

The sound of his brother's disbelief put a faint smile on Cordero's face. "That's right. I promised Jules I'd stay long enough to get Anne-Marie acquainted with the horses. It's been a while since she's ridden and Jules asked me personally to stay. I couldn't say no."

"No to him or no to this woman?" Matt asked suspiciously.

Cordero lay back on the soft duvet and stared up at the tall ceiling above his head, yet it was Anne-Marie's delicate features that swam before his eyes.

"Don't worry, Matt, Anne-Marie isn't my type of woman."

Matt grunted with even more skepticism.

"I thought any woman was your type, little brother."

That might have been true yesterday, but tonight he felt different. Tonight he was asking himself why being with Anne-Marie felt so special, why he had the feeling that he was never going to look at women in the same way again. "Not this one. She's too nice for me."

His brother let out a groan of concern. "Since when did that ever stop you?"

Frowning, Cordero said, "Look Matt, there's no need for you to keep harping at me. I'm not going to get into anything deep with Jules's daughter. I've got plenty of gals back home to keep me busy."

"Yeah. But they're here and you're there."

Chuckling now, he said, "I'll be coming home in a few days, so quit your worrying."

Matt changed the subject completely after that and Cordero was glad. He needed to remember there were other things going on in the world besides the earthquake Anne-Marie had caused inside him.

THE NEXT MORNING Cordero woke just before the sun was about to make its way through the tree limbs shading his bedroom windows. The house was quiet when he stepped into the shower and was still that way a few minutes later when he descended the stairs to the main floor.

The scent of freshly brewed coffee drifted to him and he realized that someone, more than likely Darcella, had woken up before him. He followed the smell until he found the kitchen, a long cozy room in the back of the house. Darcella was standing in front of an industrial-sized gas range where she was browning slabs of ham in an iron skillet. She glanced up and smiled as he walked over to her.

"Good mornin', Cordero. Did you sleep well enough to want breakfast?"

Once he'd turned off the lights and slipped between the sheets, he'd expected his spinning thoughts of Anne-Marie to only get worse, but the fifteen-hour drive he'd made yesterday coupled with the quietness of the plantation had worked on him as soon as his head hit the pillow. He'd slept soundly throughout the night.

"I slept great. And that ham smells delicious." He peered over the cook's shoulder and sniffed at the cooking meat. "Will there be some biscuits to go with it?"

"They're in the oven now. Would you like coffee?" she asked.

"Right now I'd give my right arm for a cup," he admitted.

Darcella laid down her turning fork and wiped her hands on the front of her thick white apron. "No need for that," she said with a smile. "You might need it to put around a pretty girl."

She turned and walked a few steps behind her to a row of oak cabinets. After she pulled a coffee cup from one of the shelves, she filled it from a coffeemaker positioned at the end of the countertop.

"Cream or sugar?" she asked.

"Black is fine."

Darcella handed him the cup and he murmured his thanks. "Mmm. This is good," he said after taking a careful sip.

With a pleased smile, Darcella went back to the stove. "Anne-Marie always tells me that I make it too strong. But she wouldn't know cause she pours in enough cream to churn butter."

"Now, Darcella, you know that isn't true. I always love your coffee."

The sound of Anne-Marie's voice surprised Cordero and he quickly turned to see her entering the kitchen through a door opening to an outside porch. She was dressed in beige jodhpurs and a starched white short-sleeved blouse that buttoned up the front. Tall English riding boots came almost to her knees and as Cordero took in her aristocratic image, he realized that his idea of riding a horse was probably going to be far different from hers.

Her gaze caught his and a smile that rivaled the dazzling sun spread across her face. The warm greeting was the last thing he'd expected from her this morning. She'd not seemed too happy with him or herself after the kiss they'd shared in the garden. When they'd parted on the staircase landing, she'd barely murmured a good-night to him. If anything, he'd expected her demeanor toward him this morning to be on the cool side.

"Good morning," she said cheerily. "I hope you're hungry. I have a table all ready for us out on the side verandah."

He gave her a lopsided grin. "I'm always hungry in the morning."

She glanced over at the cook. "Darcella is that nearly finished?"

The other woman nodded and motioned with her hand for the two of them to get out of the kitchen. "Go on. Sit. I'll bring everything in just a minute."

Anne-Marie gestured for him to follow her onto the porch. As he stepped outside he noticed this was a different side of the house than where they'd sat drinking juleps last night. This area was also screened to keep out the insects and supplied with a small group of comfortable lawn furniture. At one end, a round wooden table covered with a chintz tablecloth was set with plates and cutlery and a thermos-style coffeepot.

"You and your father must enjoy eating outdoors," Cordero remarked as he helped her into one of the cane-bottomed chairs.

"We do. Don't you eat outdoors on the Sandbur?"

His grin was wry as he seated himself in a chair angled to the right of her. "To tell you the truth, in the mornings I barely have time to gobble down an egg taco and swig a cup of coffee before I head out to work." He gestured toward the table in front of them while noticing someone had taken the trouble to place a bowl of fresh red dahlias in the middle. "I'm not used to all this. But there are occasions when we have big shindigs outside. Like my cousin's wedding reception this past weekend. And my Aunt Geraldine loves to throw parties. She can find any little reason to have a barbecue and invite the neighbors."

The smile on her face faded to a sheepish grimace. "We don't have much socializing going on here at Cane's Landing. When Mama was still alive, the place was always full of friends and neighbors. But after she died Father didn't want to entertain. Not without a hostess."

"He has you," Cordero couldn't help but point out.

The frown on her face deepened. "Yes. But I'm not...the partying sort."

There was so much going on behind that beautiful face, he concluded. He wanted to know everything she was thinking, everything that made her the woman she was now. He didn't understand this craving she'd brought about in him. He'd never cared to analyze any woman before. As long as she was warm and willing and didn't try to tie a string around his neck, he was satisfied. Why did this one fill him with one question after another?

"Why aren't you?" he asked. "Don't you like to laugh and interact with people? Have fun?"

He'd used that word more than once since she'd met him. *Fun*. The word made Anne-Marie even more certain that amusement and good times were what this man was all about. Just like Ian. When she'd first met her ex, he'd made her laugh. She'd relaxed and begun to rethink her serious attitude about life. She'd decided that maybe she was too much of a stuffed shirt and she'd tried to let herself open up and blossom. She'd thought her life was headed in the right direction, that a husband and children, a family of her own was her real calling rather than a vow to sisterhood. But then she'd learned that Ian was a phony. All he'd ever really wanted was her money and the fun he could have with it. After that, her fledgling attempt at happiness ended in a heap of humiliation.

To stifle a sigh, she sipped at her coffee. "When the fun doesn't come at someone else's expense," she said bluntly, then looked at him and attempted to give him her brightest smile. "I hope you're ready for a little riding this morning. The sky is clear and it doesn't seem too hot yet."

Before he could reply Darcella walked out on the porch carrying platters of food. He waited until the cook had placed everything onto the table and walked back into the house before he finally said, "I'm very ready to go riding. But I'm also surprised. I didn't expect you to be so cheerful this morning. Toward me or climbing on a horse."

A blush swiftly colored her face and she shrugged in an attempt to play down her obvious embarrassment. He couldn't know that she'd lain awake half the night thinking about him and wondering why she'd reacted so strongly to being in his arms. It was best he didn't know. She didn't want to add any fuel to the fire that had simmered between them in the garden.

"Look, Cordero, that kiss we shared last night—I've already put that behind me. You're only going to be here for a few days and you just implied that I should have fun. I can't see any reason why we shouldn't be friends and enjoy these coming days."

Friends. Did she really believe that prattle she'd just given him? Cordero wondered. The two of them couldn't be friends. Not after that kiss. Not after the heat he'd felt coming from her mouth and hands, the way her small curves had melted against him. But he wasn't going to point out any of that this morning. Sooner or later she would learn her mistake. Right now it was enough that she was smiling at him.

Cordero reached for a biscuit and after splitting it open began to slather the bread with fresh butter. "I'm glad you think we can be friends, Anne-Marie. It will make your father happy." His gaze lifted to her face and settled on her lips. "And me, too."

Chapter Five

The stables at Cane's Landing were located about a quarter of a mile behind the big house. Yesterday they'd left the horses in a round makeshift pen made of metal fencing that was situated on a gentle knoll in short walking distance of the horse stalls.

When Cordero and Anne-Marie approached the pen, the two gray horses perked their ears and trotted over to greet them. Anne-Marie laughed as one of them stuck his nose between the metal slats and tried to nibble her fingers.

"Taco and Lightning have been spoiled

with treats," Cordero said with a smile. "Lightning thinks you have something to give him."

Anne-Marie slid her palm over the horse's velvety nose and was surprised how drawn she was to the animal. Yesterday, when she'd helped Cordero first get the horses unloaded and settled, she'd basically tried to ignore them. Even before they'd arrived, she'd told herself she wasn't going to like them or have anything to do with them. She knew they were only pawns her father was using, and she wasn't going to play his game.

But something about Cordero made her rethink that close-minded attitude. He'd been right when he'd said it wouldn't hurt to allow Jules to manipulate them a little. Going along with her father would make him happy and perhaps keep him healthier. In the end that was the thing she wanted most.

"I should have brought them some sugar cubes," she said as she stroked her hand down the horse's nose.

Not wanting to miss the human attention, the second horse nudged his nose in beside his brother's and pushed at her hand. Anne-

Marie laughed and Cordero smiled at the pleasant sight she made.

Ben, the groundskeeper for the Duveuil homestead, had already given the horses their feed and grain for the morning, so Cordero turned toward the stables and the tack room. "You stay here and get acquainted," Cordero suggested over his shoulder to Anne-Marie. "I'll go see about finding us some saddles."

When he entered the dimly lit space, he discovered the older man was there, pushing an oil-soaked rag over a fancy tooled saddle. Faded overalls, a blue chambray shirt and laced work boots covered his tall skinny frame while a thick head of brown hair belied the fact that Anne-Marie put Ben's age near eighty. The moment he heard Cordero's step, he looked up and grinned.

"Good mornin' to you, sir. You're up and about early this mornin'." He peered curiously around Cordero's shoulder toward the door. No doubt looking for the mistress of the manor. "Is Miss Anne-Marie with you?"

Cordero nodded. "Good morning, Ben. Anne-Marie is out with the horses. I came to get the tack." He stepped over to where

Ben was working. "Looks like you've been cleaning things."

The old man's wrinkled face creased into a semblance of a smile. "Yeah. Everything in here was gettin' mighty dusty. Course, it's been a long time since anything has been used."

Cordero glanced around the room. The wooden shelves were filled with grooming and first aid products. Bits, spurs and bridles hung neatly from pegs on the wall. Saddles were carefully stacked on wooden rests. From where he stood, it looked as though the room and equipment were used every day.

"You can't tell it by looking," Cordero admitted, then turned a pointed look on the old man. "You've been doing all of this?"

Straightening to his full height, Ben tossed the rag on a nearby work counter. "Yes, sir. Feel like it's my job to take care of this stuff. Nobody else gonna do it. Mr. Jules used to help. But then Miss Fiona died and he wouldn't come down here to the stables anymore. Miss Anne-Marie rode for a while after that, but then she lost interest, too." His old face grim, he gestured to the saddles that had once been used by the people he cared about. "A sad thing to see this stuff mildew. I couldn't let it happen. Miss Fiona would be mad if she knew I sat around on my hands and let her beloved things ruin."

Sensing Ben was like many of the old wranglers on the Sandbur, Cordero knew the man was full of the past and devoted to the people who'd given him job security and a sense of family. "You knew Jules's wife well?" he asked.

He smiled fondly. "Oh yes. She was a beauty just like Miss Anne-Marie. And she was crazy about Jules—worshipped the ground he walked on. She loved horses and he bought her a whole stableful." He sighed wistfully. "Now those were the good old days. I had plenty to do to keep me busy. Horses to bathe and groom. Stalls to clean, feed and hay to spread. Nowadays I cut the grass and weed the flowers and wonder what the hell happened to this place."

Feeling for the man, Cordero reached out and patted his shoulder. "Well, I think things are about to change around here, Ben. At least you've got two horses to take care of now. Maybe they're just the first of many."

"Humph. Who's gonna ride 'em? Jules ain't young anymore and it's been so long since Anne-Marie rode she'll probably fall off."

"I wouldn't bet on that, Ben."

Both men turned around to see Anne-Marie enter the tack room. Her arms were folded against her breasts and she was staring at Ben like a teacher at an unruly child.

Undeterred, Ben reached into the front pocket of his overalls and pulled out two one-dollar bills. "This is all I have on me, but I'm bettin' Mr. Cordero here will have to pick you up off the ground before the day is over."

Straightening her shoulders, she walked over to the two men. "That'll be the day." She glanced up at Cordero's impish grin. "Unless you sold Father a couple of broncs."

Cordero laughed out loud. "Hardly. My cousin and I keep the broncs for our own amusement." His grin deepened as he winked at her. "We need a little excitement once in a while."

Apparently Ben liked the sound of that.

Slapping his leg, he laughed loudly. "That's it, Mr. Cordero. Don't let her get nothin' on you. She's spoiled, you know. She needs a firm hand."

Anne-Marie stared at the old worker with disbelief as he ambled toward the open doorway.

"Ben! What in the world has come over you?"

Without looking at her, he swatted a dismissive hand backward in her direction. "I'm just tired of it being so quiet around here. Ain't you?"

Anne-Marie's lips parted slightly as she watched the old groundskeeper slip on through the door and out of sight. His question had been a simple one, yet it caused all sorts of layered emotions to swing through her. Two days ago she'd never once thought of Cane's Landing as quiet. Maybe that was because she'd wanted to slip into the slow-moving silence and ignore the rest of the world. One thing was for certain, Cordero had invaded the place and woken her up whether she wanted it or not.

"He must be getting senile," Anne-Marie

muttered. "I told Father that Ben was getting too old for this job."

Cordero's brows lifted as he studied the faint frown on her face. "That's strange. I thought Ben was perfectly lucid and capable. In fact—" he gestured toward the neat, clean tack room "—I'd say Ben is the one who's been productive around here."

And she hadn't been? The implication of his unspoken words set her teeth together, but even as a retort came to her tongue, she quickly swallowed it down. Maybe Cordero was right. After all, what had she accomplished in the last couple of years? She'd mostly sat around and watched her father like a hawk, waiting to see if he sneezed or had the slightest twinge in his chest. Even when Jules had taken the trip to the Sandbur Ranch a couple of weeks ago, she'd not spent her free time away from the house. Her friends were limited and mostly away working for the Red Cross or some other emergency service. She was close to her cousin, who lived in Thibodaux, but Audra had a daily job and a life of her own.

"I'm glad you think someone around here is useful," she muttered, then pointed toward the saddle that the old man had been polishing. "That's the one I used to ride. Does it look okay?"

Cordero checked the latigo, girth and stirrup straps for signs of wearing or tearing. "Everything looks good. No one could tell it hadn't been used in years," he said as he looked from the saddle to her.

She let out a long breath. "I guess Ben told you that."

Cordero nodded and then, to her surprise, he touched her shoulder. "I'm sorry, Anne-Marie, that your world here at the stables died with your mother. I'd like to help you bring it back to life."

There was so much compassion in his dark eyes, so much gentle eagerness in his voice that for a moment she was overcome with emotion. Glancing away from him, she swallowed and blinked at the sting of moisture in her eyes. This was not something she was expecting from him and she didn't know how to deal with him or the feelings swirling around inside her.

After a moment, when she didn't speak, he asked, "What's the matter? Did I say something wrong?"

Forcing a smile, she turned to him and shook her head. "No. I'm just glad that you talked me into this, Cordero. I'd forgotten how much I loved horses. It would make mother happy to see me here."

Smiling gently, he slid his arm around her shoulders and squeezed her against his side. "It makes me happy to see you here, too."

Dropping her gaze from his, she reached up and absently slid her thumb and forefinger along the fold of his cotton shirt. "I'm glad you decided to stay. It's been a long time since I—since there's been anyone around for me to talk to. And ride with," she added.

She smelled like a field of flowers. Where lilac, lilies and roses nodded beneath the hot sun and their mingled scent danced on the breeze. Cordero wanted so much to kiss her that looking at her lips left him with a physical ache, but he accepted the pain and told himself to wait. Right now getting her on a horse was more important than getting her into his arms.

"Maybe you should hold judgment on that last part," he teased while easing her away from his side. "Just in case you hit the dirt like Ben has wagered."

She laughed. "I'm ready to show you both."

Laughing with her, Cordero gathered up the things they needed to dress the horses for riding. Once they had everything outside, resting on a wooden hitching post, they collected the horses and brought them to the shade beneath the shed row for saddling.

Anne-Marie helped him brush and curry the animals and place the thick blankets on their backs, but after that he shooed her out of the way. She stood to one side and watched Cordero's quick handiwork until he was ready for the last task, bridling. Then he handed one of the leather headstalls toward her.

"Go ahead. I want to see if you still remember how."

For the first time since he'd met this woman, he watched her blue eyes twinkle. "I remember. Just stand aside, cowboy."

To his surprise, she did everything right and for a moment—for a tiny split second—the idea that she would fit in his world shot through his mind like a fleeting glimpse of heaven. But just as quickly he mentally laughed at himself for entertaining such a thought, albeit briefly. Anne-Marie had her own ideas about how she wanted to spend her life and it didn't sound as though she wanted a man in it.

"Very good," he said. "Now let's see if you remember how to ride as well as you bridled."

The look on her face was somewhat provocative as she reached for the reins. She said, "I'm ready. Are you?"

He chuckled and not for the first time Anne-Marie found herself drawn to the warm husky sound.

"Let's go," he said.

They walked the two horses away from the stables to an open area. Before Cordero swung himself into the saddle, he stood behind Anne-Marie's shoulder.

"Want a hand up?" he asked.

She turned and their faces were suddenly a few inches apart. For a brief moment as his green eyes collided with her blue ones, he felt the breath rush from his lungs. The movement of her tongue as it nervously darted over her plush lips caught Cordero's gaze and held it.

"I think I can manage," she said.

Just being this close and letting his eyes drink in the lush curve of her lips, the smooth paleness of her skin, was enough to melt the buttons on his shirt. It was all he could do to keep from lifting his hand to her cheek, leaning his mouth down to hers.

"It's a long ways from the ground to Taco's back. You don't have to prove anything to me."

The corner of her lips curled up ever so slightly and it was all Cordero could do to keep from groaning out loud.

"All right. Maybe a little helping hand would be nice," she admitted.

Snatching up a handful of the horse's mane, she put her foot in the stirrup to ready herself. Cordero's first inclination was to put the palm of his hand right in the middle of her pert little rear and shove. But she'd not given him the right to be that personal so he encircled her waist with both hands and eased her gently into the seat of the saddle.

Gathering up the reins, she murmured down to him, "Thank you, Cordero."

He tipped the brim of his hat to her and then quickly swung himself into Lightning's saddle. "Which way are we going?" he asked as he nudged his horse alongside hers.

She pointed in a westerly direction. "There's an old road past the stables that will eventually lead us to the cane fields. I thought I'd give you a farming lesson today."

"All right. Lead the way."

They urged their horses into a fast walk and soon met up with the road Anne-Marie had mentioned. It was hard-packed dirt and lined with huge pecan trees and tangled underbrush. Fat squirrels raced across the path in front of them while colorful birds flitted from tree limb to tree limb.

As they ambled along, Anne-Marie, said, "This road was used by wagons and mule teams for hauling the cut cane down to the river landing. Nowadays, the tractors and harvesters have a wider, more direct path to the fields."

He glanced curiously around him. "Is that

how this place got its name? There's a river landing close by?"

She nodded. "Probably about two miles from here. I'll show you before we head home."

He caught her gaze and grinned. "Feel like kicking them into a trot?"

"Sure."

Anne-Marie was relieved to feel the horse respond immediately to the touch of her heels. But only a few seconds had passed before Cordero was calling over to her.

"You don't have to do all that posting, Anne-Marie."

"That's how I was taught to ride a trot."

"And you're doing it beautifully. But there's no need. Just put your, uh, butt down in the saddle and keep it there," he instructed.

The moment she did as he suggested, the jarring rhythm of the horse flopped her up and down and all over the seat.

"I can't—do thi—ss!" she squealed.

Laughing, Cordero moved in closer. "Yes, you can. Don't use such good posture. Slump your shoulders just a bit," he instructed. "Now, soften your spine and let it be a shock absorber."

Anne-Marie focused her entire attention on following his orders and was amazed when she felt the seat of her pants staying put.

"Cordero, look! I'm doing it, aren't I?"

He could see her smile wasn't just an expression of accomplishment. It was happy. Something he'd not seen on her face before. The sight thrilled him. This was the woman she was meant to be, he thought, with joy shining in her eyes.

"I've never seen it done better," he agreed. "And now that you've mastered that, are you ready to canter?"

"Taco's not going to bust into a buck, is he?"

Cordero laughed at her suspicious question. "No. I'd never risk that beautiful neck of yours. Come on and follow me."

Before she had time to hesitate, he kicked Lightning into a faster pace. Taco quickly followed and for the next minute or so they loped down the shady lane until the dirt path ended.

Once they pulled the animals to a stop,

Anne-Marie laughingly slid from the saddle and waited for him to dismount beside her.

"Oh, that was wonderful!" she exclaimed. "I'd forgotten how amazing it is to sit astride a horse, feeling all that power beneath you."

He'd never seen a woman look so alive or so desirable. The brown scarf that secured the hair at her nape had loosened and so had some of the copper strands. Her hair fell against her cheeks, which were flushed the color of ripe peaches. Excitement glittered in her blue eyes. All he wanted to do was gather her against him and make love to her beneath the quiet shade of the wild magnolia trees.

"See. Your father has given you a pair of wonderful gifts to enjoy," he said.

The smile slowly faded from her face. "Yes. He has." She quickly turned and led her horse away from him, over to an opening between the trees.

Cordero followed. She was looking out at acre upon acre of emerald-green sugarcane.

"Wow! That's pretty," he softly exclaimed.

The awed expression on his face surprised her. "You think so?"

He nodded. "What's not pretty about a crop growing under the hot sun? Maybe the sugar from this cane will eventually make its way to the Sandbur and Juan will make a pie from it."

A faint smile touched her lips. "Your home is far from here. Who knows what will be made from this cane. Maybe molasses for horse feed."

"Then Taco and Lightning will enjoy it," he said.

This man seemed to find something positive in everything, Anne-Marie thought. And for a moment, while they'd been cantering the horses and the wind had been whipping her cheeks, she'd felt a tiny glow of hope and renewal flickering inside of her. She'd felt a part of the happy confidence he exuded. But then he'd mentioned her father and she was suddenly reminded that Cordero was only here because of Jules. He was on this ride with her because of a sense of duty to his friend. Not because he found her wildly irresistible or because he enjoyed her company.

Annoyed with herself for thinking such

useless thoughts, she said, "Let's tether the horses and walk out in the field."

He agreed with her suggestion and after choosing a spot where the horses would be shaded, they tied the reins to a low-hanging limb and walked out between the deep furrows of plowed black dirt. Above their heads, the green cane leaves rustled slightly in the breeze.

"When will this stuff be harvested?" Cordero asked.

"Late fall. Early winter. We get one or two cuttings a year here in Louisiana before there's a chance of frost. Now if we were in Hawaii the farmers there let the cane grow for two years before it's cut. It yields a lot more sugar that way. But they have much warmer weather and a continual growing season." She reached over, broke off a stalk and stripped the leaves. "Nearly all crops are grown from seed. But cane isn't. Each harvest some of these sections are saved and planted back into the ground."

His dark brows peaked with curiosity and as she watched his face beneath the brim of his hat, she realized he was the sort of man who would always jolt a woman's senses.

She figured if she saw him fifty years from now, he'd still look just as sexy and sensual as he did today. He had that timeless sort of attraction, and it was definitely pulling on her at this very moment.

"Hmm. I didn't know that. You've taught me something. But what would happen if a flood or freeze killed the whole crop? You wouldn't have anything to replant."

She broke off a short piece of the cane and handed it to him. "Have a chew. It's sweet."

He did as she suggested and she said, "I really don't know about that part of it. You'd have to ask Father. I suppose we'd have to get pieces to plant from other cane growers."

He tossed away the piece he'd chomped on and she laughed.

"What's the matter?" she asked. "Wasn't as sweet as you thought?"

Chuckling, he reached out and snaked an arm around her waist. "It was sweet. But the dose of sugar I want is standing right here in front of me."

Taken by surprise, Anne-Marie stumbled toward him. As his hands tightened around her waist, she reached up and planted her palms against his broad chest to prevent her from falling completely against him.

"Cordero!" Tossing her head back, she stared up at his laughing face. "I told you last night that I—this wasn't going to happen again!"

The corners of his eyes crinkled with mischief. "This what? I'm not doing anything."

"Not yet. But—"

"Oh, Anne-Marie, you're too beautiful. I can't stand here with you like this and not kiss you. I wouldn't be much of a man if I didn't try, now would I?"

Her palms felt the heat of his flesh through the thin fabric of his shirt and she was horrified at how much she wanted to unbutton the fabric and slide her fingers against his chest.

Her heart thumping hard and fast, she looked down at the plowed earth beneath their feet. "Am I going to have to worry about this each time we're alone together?"

His forefinger moved beneath her chin and tilted her face up to his. "Why worry about it, Anne-Marie? Why not enjoy it?"

The warm sultry light in his dark eyes invited her to move closer, beckoned her to accept all the sinful pleasures he was offering. She tried to steel herself against the desire rising up in her, but she couldn't ignore the brush of his hard thighs next to hers, the caressing heat of his hands as they slid to the middle of her back and climbed up to her shoulders.

"You're a wicked man, Cordero." Her voice was so thick it was a struggle to get the words past her throat. "You're deliberately tempting me to cave in to you—to this!"

Grinning slyly, he leaned his forehead against hers. "Of course I'm tempting you. Because I want you."

I want you. His words tumbled over and over in her brain until erotic images of the two of them consumed her thoughts and broke the last flimsy wall of her resistance. She wanted to taste him again, feel her body crushed against his hard muscles.

The groan that sounded in her throat must have been a sign of surrender to Cordero and he took full advantage by lowering his lips to hers.

She felt herself moving forward into the solid circle of his arms, but whether she was urged on by his hands, or her own needs, she didn't know. Nor did it matter. She was where she wanted to be.

Sighing with undisguised longing, she closed her eyes and parted her lips. The bright sunshine mingled with spiky green cane leaves to create dancing colors behind her eyelids. His tongue slipped between her teeth, ventured to the roof of her mouth, then tangled with her tongue.

Sharp and sweet, desire shot straight to her core. The blood racing through her veins was like molten lava, heating every muscle, scorching every nerve in her body.

Rising on her tiptoes, she slipped her arms around his neck and pressed herself closer. The scent of him invaded her nostrils and seemed to fill every pore in her skin. The taste of his lips was like dark woodsy wine, intoxicating her, urging her to take one sip, then another and another.

Sweat rolled between her breasts and collected at her waistband. The sky above her began to spin and the ground beneath her boots felt as though it was caving away, leaving only his body to support her. Her fingers gripped his shoulders tightly. Her breathing grew so shallow it was practically nonexistent.

Somewhere in the back of her mind, Anne-Marie knew this thing between them had to end. Yet she couldn't find the strength or the will to pull away, to break the delicious spell he was weaving.

Cordero was the one who finally lifted his mouth and as he drew in several ragged breaths, Anne-Marie fought to assemble her senses. Slowly her eyelids fluttered open to see his rugged face hovering above hers. But instead of the naughty grin she expected, his expression was sober, almost haunted.

Awkwardly, she pulled her arms from his neck and splayed her palms against the middle of his chest. She could feel his heart thudding madly, matching the pulse that was pounding in her ears.

"I, uh, that was quite a kiss," he murmured.

She didn't know how her cheeks could get any hotter, but they did. Dropping her head, she turned her back to him. Even so, her maneuver didn't put any space between them. Not when his hands prevented her from moving away.

Wiping a hand at her sweaty forehead, she sighed. "It was...insane!"

His hands moved upward until they were cupping her small breasts. Anne-Marie had to bite down on her tongue to keep from groaning out loud. All she wanted was to turn and kiss him all over again. She wanted to slide her hands beneath his shirt, feel his skin slick against hers, his body driving into her.

Bending his head, he whispered, "Then it was a sweet insanity."

The touch of his lips against the soft curve of her neck splintered her resistance and her head lolled backward until it rested against his shoulder.

"I'm not your plaything, Cordero."

His fingers began to knead the soft flesh of her breasts. "No. You're a woman who's been lonely. A woman who's been trying to pretend she doesn't need a man's arms around her."

Not willing to accept anything he was saying, she twisted away. As she went, his hand caught the scarf slipping from her hair and before she could get away entirely, he used the silk as a snare around her waist.

As he tugged her back to him, she said in a flustered voice, "You don't know what I want or need!"

"Then I guess I'll just have to show you all over again," he drawled as she landed with a thump against his chest.

Chapter Six

Anne-Marie was desperately wondering where she would find the strength to survive another one of his kisses when suddenly the rumbling sound of a tractor could be heard on the opposite end of the field.

With a wry smile, Cordero handed her the scarf and allowed her to step away from him.

"Great timing," he muttered.

Her hands shaking, she struggled to tie the scarf around her tumbled hair. "One of the hands must be checking the crops for insects or fungus."

Realizing the intimate moments between them were over, he placed his hand against her back and urged her out of the cane field. "Let's get back to the horses," he said.

Once they reached Taco and Lightning, they untied the horses and Cordero helped Anne-Marie climb into the saddle.

Without looking at him, she said, "I can do it myself."

"Don't be silly. We were close to making love a few moments ago. It won't change anything if I touch you now."

Her lips were set in a grim line as she glanced over her shoulder at him. "All right, but then we're going straight home."

Instead of putting his hands on her waist to lift her up, his fingers closed around her shoulders and slowly turned her toward him.

"Why do you want to go back home?" he asked softly. "So you can hide from me? And yourself?"

"That's an awful thing to say."

"No, it's an awful thing for you to do."

She let out a long breath as all sorts of emotions warred inside her. "I'm not trying to hide. I just want to—"

When she didn't go on, he finished for

her, "Play it safe? Isn't that what you're try-ing to say?"

Annoyed with herself, she said, "What if I am? There's nothing wrong with trying to keep a sensible head."

Groaning with disbelief, he brushed his fingers tenderly against her cheek. "Oh, Anne-Marie, I don't know where you got this idea that you need to live such a pure, solitary life, but it's not for you. You were made for a man to love and for you to love him in return."

Swallowing at the tightness in her throat, she turned her gaze toward Taco's gray dappled shoulder. "My lot is to help others, Cordero. Why can't you accept that?"

Because he'd tasted the passion in her kiss, the need in her clinging hands. In fact, he could still feel the soft shape of her lips beneath his, the way her small body had melted against him. Kissing her hadn't just left him with a burning ache, it had shattered something deep inside him and left him feeling exposed and vulnerable. A kiss wasn't supposed to do all that.

"You can help others and still have a man in your life."

Her blue eyes searched his face. "Is that what you're trying to be? The man in my life?"

Cordero didn't know what the hell he was trying to do, other than assuage the itch to make love to her. Yet touching her, even in a casual way, was turning out to be worse than shoving his hand into the branding fire. Kissing her had burned him right down to the bone. What would having sex with her do to him? Turn him into a pile of useless ashes?

"I don't know. Maybe."

"Liar," she said softly. "You're trying to convince me that there would be nothing wrong in having sex with you."

Cordero couldn't remember the last time he'd blushed. Maybe in grade school when his teacher had called on him to read a soppy love poem in front of the class. But now he could feel red heat climbing up his face and stinging his jaws.

"There wouldn't be. I mean—anything wrong—with you and me—together."

Anne-Marie rolled her eyes. "Maybe not for you. But it would be for me." With a shake of her head, she confessed, "I've never met a man like you, Cordero."

His gaze soft upon her face, he trailed a finger down the side of her cheek. "I'm glad. I don't think the world could handle two of us."

She certainly doubted it. She couldn't even handle one of him.

With a soft little sigh, she turned her back to him and lifted her foot to the stirrup. "Come on," she said, "help me up. And I'll show you the river landing."

His hands closed around her slender waist, but instead of lifting her into the saddle, he brought his lips near her ear.

"Thank you, Anne-Marie."

His murmured words confused her and she turned her head just enough to catch a glimpse of his face. "For what?" she asked.

"Not running away from me."

There was no teasing in his voice, only a raw longing that made everything inside Anne-Marie want to turn and fling herself into his arms.

Instead, she merely nodded and waited for the lift of his strong hands to help her into the saddle.

LATER THAT MORNING, when they returned to the homestead, Audra Duveuil was sitting on the front porch, drinking iced lemonade and scratching Lucy between the ears. As soon as the hound spotted Anne-Marie and Cordero walking toward the house, she ran out in a fit of whines and wiggles to greet them. On the porch, Audra rose to her feet and smiled.

Unlike Anne-Marie, Audra was tall and slender with hair the color of onyx and eyes nearly as dark. At the age of thirty, she'd been divorced for five years and did her best to pretend that she was perfectly content to live alone.

"I was wondering if you'd gotten lost," she exclaimed as Anne-Marie and Cordero climbed the steps.

Anne-Marie left Cordero's side to go to her cousin. "What a surprise," she murmured as she kissed the other woman's cheek. "I didn't know you were coming."

Audra chuckled. "I wanted to surprise you. I didn't have to go in to work today, so I thought I'd come out and see what was happening on the plantation. I didn't realize you had company until Darcella told me."

Anne-Marie quickly motioned for him to join them. "Cordero, this is my cousin Audra. The one that lives in Thibodaux."

With a charming smile, Cordero swept off his Stetson and extended his hand to the woman. "Very nice to meet you, Audra. So you're the cousin with the smart brother."

Audra glanced with faint surprise at Anne-Marie, before she smiled at Cordero. "That's right. Anne-Marie must have been talking about her relatives."

"Believe me, it was all nice talk," he said as he slowly dropped her hand.

"Darcella tells me you're from Texas," Audra replied. "I hope you're enjoying your stay here in Louisiana."

Anne-Marie felt him glance her way.

"Every minute, thank you," he told her, then quickly added. "I'll leave you two ladies alone so that you can visit. I have several phone calls to make."

He quickly excused himself and both women watched him go into the house before either one of them spoke.

"Whew!" Audra exclaimed as she sank back into the lawn chair. "What a man! Darcella wasn't kidding when she told me he was sexy."

Normally it never bothered Anne-Marie when her cousin spoke her mind. But for some reason Audra's blatant gushing over Cordero annoyed her.

"Darcella thinks any man under eighty is sexy," Anne-Marie mumbled as she sat in a chair that faced her cousin's. As she bent forward and unbuckled her spurs, she added, "And Cordero is Father's friend. Not mine."

Audra's chuckles were skeptical. "When you two were walking up here a moment ago, you looked pretty chummy to me."

Frowning, Anne-Marie looked up at her. "Just because he's gentleman enough to offer me his arm? Really, Audra, you should have been a writer. Your imagination is overactive."

Not a bit bothered by her cousin's sarcasm, Audra sighed. "Okay, so he's not your friend. He's just a houseguest."

Anne-Marie pulled the tiny spurs from her boot heels, then straightened back in her seat. Without even glancing Audra's way, she knew her cousin was taking in her tumbled hair and swollen lips. Drat it. Of all the times for her to show up, it had to be this morning.

"That's right," Anne-Marie said primly. "And since Father is still in the hospital, I'm merely acting as hostess."

Audra sighed wistfully as she picked up her glass of lemonade. "If only I could be so lucky."

Anne-Marie darted a glare at her. "What are you talking about? You haven't dated in years. Not since you and Doug got divorced. Don't tell me you're pining for male company. I wouldn't believe it."

Audra rolled her eyes. "If the company looked like your Cordero I certainly might consider it," she said in a teasing voice, then batted a dismissive hand through the air. "But that's not important. How is Jules?"

Grateful that the other woman was going to get off the subject of Cordero, Anne-Marie leaned back in her chair and shook her hair loose of the brown scarf. "Thankfully he's doing well. I talked to him this morning before breakfast. He actually sounded chipper. And he expects the doctor to be finished with all the tests by the end of the week. He'll probably be releasing him from the hospital then."

"Good," Audra replied, then after a sip of lemonade she added, "Actually, I went by the hospital yesterday morning to see Uncle Jules. If I hadn't known better, I would've thought the man was as well as you or I."

"Well, we're not doctors or nurses," Anne-Marie reasoned. "In any case, I hope you're right."

Over the rim of her glass, Audra thoughtfully studied her. "I hope I am, too. Maybe you'll finally decide your father is well enough for you to get back to the land of the living."

Anne-Marie stiffened. She wasn't in the mood for a lecture from Audra. As much as she loved her cousin, they were as opposite as night and day. Audra had a high-paying job as a secretary to a prominent lawyer in New Orleans. She loved all the luxuries her father's inheritance had given her and made no attempt to hide it. Whereas, Anne-Marie had often wished she'd been born into a poor family. At least then she would know that people wanted to be with her just for herself and not her money.

She'd been a naive fool for ever letting Ian into her life. But he'd been so charming and smooth and had presented himself as a man of integrity. Instead, he'd been a fake, a con out to find himself a rich wife to make his life easy. He'd lied about coming from a respected family in South Carolina. He'd lied about going to medical school. And, most of all, he'd lied about loving her.

"I don't want to hear it, Audra. Not today."

"Don't get all angry with me, honey. It's just that I worry about you." She shook her head with disbelief. "I'd rather see you traipsing around in some muddy jungle handing out boxes of food and jugs of water to the needy than to see you hiding yourself away here on Cane's Landing."

Anne-Marie turned around in her chair so that she was facing her cousin head-on. "I can't think of a more beautiful place to be than Cane's Landing."

Crossing her long legs, Audra restlessly tapped the toe of her high-heeled sandal. "It is lovely here. And it would be the perfect place for you if—" she cut her eyes toward the front door of the house "—that sexy cowboy was here to share it with you."

"Oh my word, Audra," Anne-Marie said under her breath. "You're out of your mind. Cordero lives on a rich ranch out in Texas. He has a big family there. And he's not in the market for marriage or anything like it. Neither am I."

Audra let out another wistful sigh. "Okay. So I'll do the dreaming for you, honey."

Anne-Marie slid the brown scarf through her fingers and tried not to think how Cordero had used it to rope her back into his arms. Touching him, kissing him had shaken everything inside her. He'd not only left her burning with desire, but he'd left her wanting to snuggle in the shelter of his arms, to be protected and comforted. The unexpected emotions had troubled her—were still troubling her.

"So did you drop by for some reason other than to scold me?" Anne-Marie asked pointedly.

Audra smiled. "Actually, I came over to invite you out tonight for supper and a movie. They're showing some classic film noir at the Balfour this month. Tonight is Bogart night."

Anne-Marie shifted uncomfortably in her chair. "Sounds good, but I can't. I've promised Father to take Cordero to New Orleans for supper and a little jazz."

Audra's black brows shot upward. "You're kidding! You're actually going out on a date with the man? To Bourbon Street!"

Frowning, Anne-Marie rose to her feet. "No. I didn't say anything about a date. I'm merely acting as hostess, remember? And what's so shocking about me going to Bourbon Street? That's where fallen angels go, isn't it?" she asked sardonically, then started toward the door. "Come on, let's go in. I need to change and get something to drink."

After fetching a glass of ice water from the kitchen, Audra followed Anne-Marie upstairs to her bedroom. While her cousin lounged on the bed, Anne-Marie stood behind a dressing screen and changed into jeans and a T-shirt.

"Darcella told me that you and Cordero had gone riding," Audra commented. "I'm so glad that Uncle Jules bought the horses.

It's about time you got interested in them again. Aunt Fiona would be so happy."

Shoving her feet into a pair of leather thongs, Anne-Marie stepped from behind the screen. "Yes, I suppose she would be. But Mama was the sort that—well, she was so rounded. She was good at everything."

Frowning slightly, Audra rolled onto her side and stared out the window. "When are you ever going to realize that Fiona wasn't a saint, Anne-Marie? And you're not, either. You're a flesh-and-blood woman. I wish you'd start acting like one."

Pensively, Anne-Marie walked around the bed to stand at the window. Below them was the backyard garden where Cordero had kissed her. The memory of that moment was still so ripe in her mind that merely thinking of it made her bite down on her lip to keep from groaning aloud. As she stared down at the cherub pouring water from his jug, she murmured, "Cordero got the feeling, Audra."

"Hmm? What are you talking about?"

"You know. In the garden. I've told you about it before—that sense of presence, Mama's spirit. Cordero felt it."

Audra scooted to a cross-legged position in the middle of the bed and looked at her with faint surprise. "You mean after you told him about it?"

"No. I hadn't said anything. He kept looking around the garden and said he felt as though someone was there, watching us. It really took me by surprise. No one but me has ever felt it. I wonder—what could it mean?"

Audra shrugged. "I don't know. The man doesn't look the spiritual sort to me."

Shaking her head, Anne-Marie continued to stare down at the fountain. "I think you're wrong about that, Audra. For more than two years, Cordero's father was handicapped with a brain injury. He never lost faith that his father would one day be better. And he was right, his father is well now." She sighed. "I'm not sure I still have that depth of faith."

"Well hell, how could you?" Audra practically snorted. "That cracker, Ian, broke your heart. You lost faith in men, yourself, even God. But you'll get it back, sweetheart."

Yes, Anne-Marie thought desperately, she would get it all back. She had to. As Cordero had said, she couldn't keep running and hiding from life.

She heard the bedclothes rustle and looked around to see Audra walking over to a large, intricately carved armoire.

"Come on," she said, "that's enough dark talk. Let's pick out something for you to wear tonight. I think it should be something sizzling. You still have that skinny thing with the spaghetti straps that I gave you for Christmas?"

Anne-Marie rushed over to where Audra was busily pushing garments back and forth across the metal rack.

"Not that red thing! It shows way too much cleavage. I've never worn it and I definitely won't wear it tonight!"

Audra chuckled as she found the dress she was searching for and pulled it from the armoire. "Why not? I'm sure your Texas cowboy would love it."

That was exactly what Anne-Marie was afraid of. "Forget it, Audra. I'm not dressing for him tonight."

LATER THAT EVENING, long after her cousin had left the plantation, Anne-Marie stood in front of the cheval glass in her bedroom and stared at the image before her.

The red dress fit her slender body to just below the curve of her bottom, then flared into graceful swirls around her knees. The bodice was covered with thin chiffon tucked into tiny pleats, yet Anne-Marie couldn't appreciate the fine fabric or the detailed tailoring. Her gaze was fixed upon the faint slope of her breasts that was bared above the straight neckline.

On anyone else the dress wouldn't seem all that provocative; it only hinted at the body beneath. But on her, it appeared scandalous. Or was that simply because she'd never allowed herself to wear such clothing?

Thoughtfully, her hand drifted up to the single strand of pearls lying against her chest. She did look nice, even sexy, she decided, and the knowledge thrilled her in a way she didn't understand. Is that what Cordero was doing to her? Making a part of her long to be a sexual, sensual siren? Even Ian hadn't given her the urge to wear a dress like this.

She was wondering what that could possibly mean, when a light knock sounded on the bedroom door. Darcella stuck her head around the panel of wood. "Jules is on the phone. He wants to speak to you," she said, then seeing Anne-Marie in the red dress, she stepped into the room.

Anne-Marie turned to face her and Darcella gave her a broad smile of approval. "I've never seen anyone more beautiful than you are right now, honey. My, oh my, that cowboy is gonna have his eyes full tonight."

"You're the closest thing I have to a mother, Darcella," Anne-Marie said soberly. "So be truthful with me. Do I look like a…harlot?"

Darcella closed the short distance between them and clasped Anne-Marie's face between her work-worn hands. "Don't you ever talk that way 'bout yourself, Anne-Marie! You're a lovely young woman. You look just like you're supposed to look—*finally*. I only wish Jules could see you." She dropped her hands and motioned for the telephone on the nightstand. "You better get the phone. We'll talk later."

As the cook left the room, Anne-Marie walked over and picked up the portable telephone. "Hello, Father."

"Sweetheart, I thought you were going to call this evening. Is everything okay?"

Clutching the phone to her ear, Anne-Marie sank onto the edge of the bed. "Everything is fine. I was just about to call you. I've been busy getting ready to go over to New Orleans."

She could hear Jules sigh with something suspiciously close to relief.

"So you're not trying to make up some excuse to stay home?"

Anne-Marie passed a hand over her skirt. The slinky fabric felt smooth as it slipped across her skin, but it couldn't compare to the sensation of Cordero's palm gliding across her back. "No. I'm actually looking forward to it. So is Cordero."

"Good! That's the best medicine I've had today! So you two are getting along okay?"

Suddenly Anne-Marie was standing back in the tall cane with her eyes closed against the morning sun and Cordero's lips rocking over hers.

She swallowed. "Uh, yes. No problems. He's been very nice. And we had a pleasant ride this morning. I rode Taco. He's beautiful and affectionate and very well mannered. I—oh, Father, I'm so glad you didn't listen to me. I love the horses. I only wished you hadn't spent so much money—"

"Nonsense!" he interrupted, his voice gruffly covering his emotion. "You're all I have, honey. Don't deprive me of the joy of spoiling you just a little. Besides, Cordero has spent many hours training those horses. They're worth every penny I paid for them—especially if you're happy with them."

She was happy. Whether the upbeat feeling in her heart was from being with horses again, or from Cordero's company, she didn't know. Nor was she going to start analyzing the question this evening. She was simply thankful that the dark weight she'd been carrying around for so long now seemed to be lifting.

"How are you feeling, Father? What does the doctor say?"

"I'm feeling like a young rooster. No need to worry about me. Doc says he still has three or four more tests to do and then he'll turn me loose."

"Three or four!" she exclaimed with disbelief. "What could he possibly have left to do to you? There're only so many tests that can be run. Maybe I should speak to him."

"No! I mean—there's no need for that. Doc knows what he's doing. You know, honey, he wants to take all sorts of pictures of my ticker while I'm resting and walking. It's nothing to get alarmed about. He says everything is checking out just great."

"Hmm. Well, that's wonderful news. But it would be nice if you could get out of the hospital before Cordero went home. I know you two had planned on doing things together."

"Never you mind that. Cordero isn't blind. He'd much rather have a few days with a pretty lady like you than an old crank like me. Now you just put your mind to rest about your father and go enjoy yourself tonight."

Anne-Marie assured him that she'd do her best to show Cordero a pleasant evening, then quickly gave him her love and hung up. She'd just put the telephone back on its cradle and picked up her evening bag when another knock sounded on the door. This time she found Cordero standing on the other side and, for a moment, the sight of him stunned her into silence.

Starched jeans and a white long-sleeved shirt covered his long, lean body. Except for a wayward lock that had fallen near his temple, his black hair, still damp from a shower, was combed straight back from his forehead. He smelled like sweet grasses and dark musk and the sexy curve to the corner of his lips made something in her stomach twist into an aching knot.

"Hi, beautiful."

Anne-Marie's first instinct was to glance over her shoulder to make sure he wasn't seeing an apparition behind her. When she realized his words were actually meant for her, a blush formed on her cheeks.

In nervous reaction, her fingers lifted to her upswept hair and fiddled with a pearl and rhinestone clasp embedded in the red waves. "Hi, yourself. Ready to go?"

He nodded while his gaze swept down to her strapped high heels and back up to the top of her hair. "You certainly look as though you're ready." His lips spread into a wide grin as he reached for her hand. "Come here and let me see you."

Pulling her out onto the landing, he twirled her around as though they were on the dance floor. Anne-Marie suddenly found herself giggling, something she could never remember doing before.

"Cordero! This is crazy. You're crazy!"

Laughing along with her, he slipped his arm around her and guided her down the curved staircase. Anne-Marie wondered if this was how it felt to step into a fairy tale. Cordero was certainly equal to any Prince Charming she'd ever read about.

Once they reached the living room, Darcella saw them off. She followed them onto the porch and waited long enough to wave as they drove away.

"I think she's happy to see us go," Cordero said as he steered the car down the oak-lined lane.

Anne-Marie smiled. "She's happy because she doesn't have to cook supper tonight."

"Poor woman. My being here has put an extra burden on her."

"Don't be silly. I was only teasing. If I were visiting the Sandbur you wouldn't think I was burdening your cook, would you?"

He laughed. "Not hardly. There are always plenty of people around to eat. You'd just be one more mouth to feed." He arched a curious brow her way. "Why? Are you thinking of coming for a visit?"

She plucked at the hem of her skirt. "Maybe someday."

They reached the end of the long lane and, after coming to a careful stop, Cordero turned the car onto the road.

"Why not soon? You'd like it, I promise. We have about two hundred horses, give or take a foal or two and thousands of acres. You could come at roundup time in the spring and see what it's like to gather cattle and eat off a chuck wagon."

Her sigh was a bit wistful. "You make it sound like a wonderful adventure."

He glanced at her. "I guess *you'd* say it's an adventure. I certainly wouldn't want to live anywhere else."

No, Anne-Marie thought, Cordero was a born-and-bred Texan. He wouldn't leave his ranch for anything. Not even for a woman.

She was staring pensively out the window when he reached over and picked up her hand. Turning her head, she watched in wary fascination as he lifted her fingers to his lips.

"But for the next few days I wouldn't want to be anywhere else, except right here with you."

Next few days. Yes, she thought with a strange sense of sadness. In a few days Cordero would be gone. The sound of his laughter and his soft Texas drawl would no longer fill the empty rooms at Cane's Landing. And she'd put away this red dress she was wearing. Probably forever.

Chapter Seven

The drive to New Orleans took forty-five minutes. By the time they entered the city, the sun had fallen and dusk was spreading shadows along the busy streets.

They found a safe parking place before hailing a taxi to the French Quarter. Along the way, the driver advised them of several places to eat, but Cordero had ideas of his own.

When they stepped onto the sidewalk and began to stroll between the Creole-style buildings, he said, "Let's not eat in some stuffy place. I didn't wear a jacket. I probably couldn't get in anyway. Do you mind?"

His hand was curved against her shoulder, his fingers lightly splayed against her upper arm. The warmth of his touch was like a sunbeam, lifting her spirits, making her feel as though her feet were barely skimming the ground.

She smiled up at him. "Of course not. This is your night on the town. You pick the spot."

Laughing, he urged her down the sidewalk. "An unselfish woman. You're a rare specimen, Anne-Marie."

No, he was the rare one, she thought. He made her feel special. Snuggled next to his side, she could almost forget that she'd allowed an immoral man to lead her astray, to forever change the sacred direction of her life.

They walked for several blocks, through crowds that thickened as soon as night began to fall upon the crescent city. Music and laughter could be heard on every street corner while the smells of spicy Creole and Cajun cooking permeated the air.

Eventually they found a small restaurant

with the front door propped open and a sign hanging from the awning that simply read: Good Food. Est. 1865. Blues music, along with the smell of fried oysters, drifted out to them.

"Well, if the place has lasted this long, it must be good," Cordero said with a laugh. "Are you game?"

A week ago, even a day ago, Anne-Marie would have considered the eating place a bit seedy for her taste. But tonight, with Cordero by her side, his impish grin urging her on, she felt the fun of trying something new.

"Sure," she said. "Let's go in."

With his arm at her back, he guided her into the dimly lit café. Someone behind a short, busy bar yelled, "Seat yourself. Anywhere you like."

The room was L-shaped with the front part running adjacent to the sidewalk. Cordero ushered her to the only empty table he could find, which was situated near the paned windows looking out at the street.

After he seated her in one of the old, rope-bottomed chairs and took his place beside her at the small, round table, Cordero realized that the music was coming from a CD player sitting at the end of the bar. Customers, varying from young adults to very old seniors were talking, laughing and eating from platters of food. Some of them were loud and some were dressed in work clothes right off the construction site, but all appeared to be enjoying themselves.

They'd hardly gotten settled when a waiter appeared and Cordero ordered wine for both of them. After that they began their meal with turtle soup, then moved on to fried frog legs. By the time they were served a dessert of rum-soaked bread pudding, Anne-Marie was totally stuffed and mellow from the wine and relaxed atmosphere.

"This is absolutely delicious, but I don't think I can eat another bite," she said with a contented groan.

"What about coffee?"

"Mmm. Sounds good. But I don't think I could hold another sip of anything."

Cordero placed his fork on his nearly empty plate. "I'm stuffed, too. We'll get coffee later. And I know just the place to do it. Are you ready to go?"

Her brows peaked with interest. "You have a certain place you want to go? I thought I was taking you to listen to some jazz or blues music."

Grinning, he leaned his head toward hers and whispered. "I don't want you to hear any songs about women wronged by no-account men. I want to put a smile on your face."

He touched the pad of his forefinger to the faint dimple in the middle of her chin. Anne-Marie's eyes were drawn to his. As she looked into their hazel depths the sounds of music and voices and clatter from the kitchen all faded away. Her breath caught in her throat and for a brief moment she forgot that they were in a public place.

Closing her eyes, she leaned forward just enough to touch her lips to his. With his thumb and finger lightly grasping her chin, he parted his lips and kissed her softly and swiftly. The fleeting taste of him whetted her appetite for more and she sighed with longing when he pulled his head away.

"Let's go," he murmured. Rising to his feet, he offered his hand to help her from her seat.

Anne-Marie waited near the entrance while Cordero took care of the bill. When they stepped outside, the street was dark and the steamy night air drifted around them like hot fog. Cordero took her by the arm and led her to the curb.

"Let's see if we can catch a cab," he told her.

"You mean we can't walk to where we're going?" she asked with surprise.

He grinned down at her. "No."

Her brows lifted. "Where is this place? Or should I ask *what* is it?"

He chuckled as he raised his arm and beckoned an approaching cab. "Don't be so nosy," he said teasingly. "You'll find out when we get there."

Fifteen minutes later, when Anne-Marie looked up and down the cracked sidewalk, she had no idea what part of the city they were in. Both sides of the street were lined by dark, empty warehouses. Except for the one they were standing in front of. Lights streamed from the windows high above them, while below several people entered and exited.

Cordero ushered her through the double doors. "They have delicious food here. But since we've already eaten, we'll just have something to drink and enjoy the music. Do you like to dance?"

"D-ance?" she sputtered. Anne-Marie hadn't danced since junior high and she'd only danced then because it had been a part of a music class assignment. "I'm not a dancer, Cordero! If you brought me here for that, you've wasted your time and cab fare."

Frowning, he brought his arm around her shoulders and guided her through the crowd. "Nonsense!" he scoffed. "All women know how to dance. You were made for it."

No, she was made to travel to spots in the world where natural disasters had occurred. To aid people who were homeless, hungry and lost. She was meant to walk a narrow, righteous path and be even more virtuous than her own mother had been. For years those were the things Anne-Marie had envisioned for her future. Even her brief infatuation for Ian hadn't totally wiped those plans from her mind. Yet Cordero was demolishing that narrow path she'd set for herself. Just being in his presence was opening up new horizons, filling her head with all sorts of possibilities. Could he be right? Was she really meant to be a wife? A mother? A lover?

Tonight was not the time to be asking herself those questions, she told herself, as they found a tiny table at the back of the dance floor. Cordero was showing her a glimpse of his brand of entertainment and she wanted to learn everything she could about him before he eventually told her goodbye.

While they waited for the waitress to bring their coffee, Anne-Marie turned her attention to the far corner of the room, where a large nautical rope cordoned off a six-piece band from the dancers and diners. The lively Cajun music was infectious and she found herself tapping her toes to the beat.

"How did you know about this place?" she asked slyly.

A smug grin crossed his face. "I came here with my cousin Lex a couple of years ago. We were here in town for a horse and cattle breeder's convention. I don't know how he knew about the place. But since Lex has a girlfriend in every port, so to speak, it's not hard to figure out how he became familiar with this nightspot. Lex, uh, gets around."

As he spoke, she was amazed at how much she wanted to run her finger along his sideburn, down his jaw and across his lips. Just the thought made her shiver.

"It sounds as though you're close to your cousin. Are you?"

The waitress appeared with their coffee. After she'd placed the steaming mugs onto the little table and left, Cordero said, "Lex is more like a brother than a cousin. We were both raised on the Sandbur and have never lived anywhere else."

"Is he your age?"

"Four years older. When we were just kids he and my brother, Matt, used to give me a hard time for wanting to tag along with them. Lex used to fancy himself a saddle bronc rider and traveled the rodeo circuit some back in his younger days." Smiling with fond remembrance, he lifted the coffee cup to his lips. "He was my hero and I wanted to be just like him. Until I figured out that having your nose buried in arena dirt didn't feel all that glorious."

Anne-Marie smiled. "I can't imagine you ever being bucked off a horse."

He laughed. "Boy, I must have you horn-swoggled. I couldn't count the times I've found myself looking up at the sky or seeing hooves stomping around my head. Each horse is different and the young ones are always unpredictable when you start breaking them to the saddle."

She scanned his face as she took a careful sip of coffee. "You really like what you do, don't you?"

Another smile creased his cheeks. "It beats getting a real job."

He was teasing, of course. Anne-Marie knew enough about horses to know that his job required long exhausting hours and plenty of skill, both mental and physical. A good horse trainer had to have an innate sense of what the animal was thinking and how to communicate with it.

"I can tell by the way Taco and Lightning behave that you're good at what you do," she said.

To her surprise, he seemed a bit embarrassed by her compliment. His gaze dropped to the tabletop as he shrugged one shoulder.

"I've got a long way to go to ever be as good as my father," he said quietly.

And Anne-Marie was far from being as good a woman as her mother had been, she thought dismally. She'd tried, but she'd failed.

"I'm sure you're being modest now."

With a wry twist to his lips, Cordero lifted his gaze back to her face. He'd not expected to hear such praise from Anne-Marie. But then all this evening she'd been surprising him. Especially with that little kiss she'd given him in the café. The simple overture had knocked him sideways. Was she trying to tell him that she wanted him?

Ever since they'd left the French Quarter, he'd been telling himself not to dwell on that tiny meeting of lips. But forgetting was a hard thing to do when she looked like a vision in red.

Reaching across the table, he slipped a forefinger across her collarbone. "You look lovely tonight, Anne-Marie." Too lovely, he thought. The sight of her pale skin against the vivid dress was like cream against cherries. He wanted to touch and taste. He wanted to slip his fingers into the curls piled atop her head, pull the pins and watch the heavy waves fall around her shoulders. But more than anything he wanted to take her home to the plantation and make love to her. Did she want the same things? There were fleeting moments when he thought he saw longing in her eyes. But maybe he was only seeing the mirror of his own feelings.

"Thank you," she murmured.

He pushed the coffee cup away and reached for her hand. "Come on. The night's wasting and we haven't danced yet."

Her eyes widened with something close to panic as he pulled her from her seat. "Cordero! I told you that I don't know how!"

"Then I'll teach you," he said with a wicked grin.

At the edge of the crowded dance floor, he threaded one hand through hers and snagged her waist with the other.

"Just follow me," he urged. "It's a quick round dance. You can do it."

Anne-Marie let out a sound that was a groan and a laugh mixed together. "Yeah, that's easy enough for you to say, Mr. Astaire. Just don't yell if I trip or smash your toes."

The loud zydeco number drowned out his laughter, but she could see the deep amusement on his face as he put them into a quick pace across the wooden parquet. At first she was so worried about keeping up with him without tangling her feet that she concentrated solely on putting her feet in the right spot. But that focus quickly faded as the fast steps, the infectious music and the sight of Cordero's happy face filled her with a joy that bubbled up inside her like a fizzy drink. By the middle of the second song, she was laughing and twirling beneath Cordero's arm as though she'd done it a thousand times before.

They danced several fast songs in a row, only stopping long enough to catch their breath while the band paused then started again. But then the music changed to a slow, sweet Cajun number sung in French. Cordero pulled Anne-Marie close against him and dipped his cheek next to hers.

"Finally. I get a reason to have you in my arms," he murmured.

His drawl sent a pleasant shiver down her spine. "I've never done anything like this before, Cordero. I never thought—" she tilted her head so that she could see his face "—it would be this nice."

His hand moved from her waist to her shoulders. As his fingers made lazy, sensual circles against her bare skin, she fought the urge to close her eyes and press her face against the middle of his chest.

"I'm glad you're having a good time," he said. "See, your father isn't so senile after all."

A smile touched her lips. "To be honest, it shocks me that you turned out to be his friend."

"Why?" he asked comically. "What's wrong with me?"

She chuckled. "Darcella and I thought you were going to be an older man. Like in your sixties or seventies. And then when it turned out to be you—well, I couldn't imagine you and Father even having a conversation, much less being friends. Most men your age wouldn't bother to say two words to someone like Jules."

He frowned down at her. "Then that would be their loss. I have plenty of buddies my own age, but older friends are like having a taste of aged wine—a lot more substance to it, you know."

"Well, I thank you for being so...indulgent with Father. It means very much to me."

Bending his head, he rubbed his cheek against hers. "It's my pleasure, Anne-Marie."

Something was happening to her, she thought, as they slowly circled through the crowd of dancers. Layer by layer this man was tearing away all the protective cloaks she'd gathered around her, yanking the dark shadows from her heart. For the first time since her ordeal with Ian, she wanted to live and feel like a woman again.

"This song is beautiful," he mused out loud. "I wish I could understand the words."

His comment interrupted her thoughts and turned her attention to the lyrics, which were as haunting as the melody.

After a moment, she said, "She's singing about her lover. He's left her and she can't decide if she should go after him."

"Oh."

His simple reply was just awkward enough to tell Anne-Marie that he wasn't comfortable with the subject of love between a man and a woman. It also told her that he would never want a woman chasing after him. He valued his independence too much.

That thought took the joy out of the night. Which was silly. He'd only said one word. She was probably reading too much into it. Besides, she wasn't serious about Cordero. She wasn't thinking of him as a husband, a long-term lover, or any of those things. Still, the evening had somehow lost its luster so she suggested it was getting late enough that they should head home.

To her surprise he didn't argue and they quickly left the warehouse.

A half hour later, they were back in her car, traveling north out of the city. Dancing with Cordero had left Anne-Marie in a dreamy state of mind and the strange emotions she'd felt in his arms were still occupying her mind as the car sped homeward.

As she rested her head against the back of the seat, staring silently out at the black night, Cordero's husky voice penetrated the silence that had settled around them. Yet it was not the sound of his voice that grabbed her attention. His question was what had her turning her head and staring at him with frank surprise.

"What happened with you and…the man you told me about? Why did your relationship end?"

Ian was not a subject she discussed with anyone. Not even with Audra or her father. Once she'd ended the relationship, she'd not said any more. In her opinion, he'd not been worth the time or the effort. Yet Cordero's question had been asked in a sincere way and after tonight she couldn't refuse him. Perhaps a part of her even *wanted* to confide in him, share with him.

Straightening in her seat, she sighed. "I think maybe I should first explain how we met. Otherwise, you won't get the whole picture."

He inclined his head. "Tell me. I want to know."

She drew in a ragged breath and let it out. "I met Ian at Saint Mary's, our family church. He showed up at service one Sunday morning and introduced himself to the congregation saying he was from South Carolina and that he was making his way across the United States doing missionary work. He was my age, good-looking and charming in a quiet way. Everybody liked him and exclaimed over his good works in the church. He volunteered for all sorts of charity activities and was always ready to help."

"Sounds too good to be true."

Anne-Marie grimaced. "You're right. Of course no one knew that at first—except Father. He had his suspicions. And I guess I didn't want to believe him. I thought he was simply trying to find fault with Ian because he was being protective."

Cordero glanced at her. "So why did you start dating the guy if you were planning on entering a convent? I don't understand."

With a shameful groan, Anne-Marie passed a hand over her face. "Oh, Cordero, I'm sure you've seduced a woman before. Well, Ian set out to seduce me. Only I didn't see it coming. I was innocent and naive. By the time I fell in love with him, I had convinced myself that God had chosen a different path for me. I thought marrying Ian and helping him with missionary activities would be just as meaningful."

Staring at the highway in front of them,

Cordero said, "I see. So you loved this man? You wanted to marry him?"

Another sigh slipped past Anne-Marie's lips. "At that time I believed I did. But I... now I think I was simply infatuated with him and with the idea of having a wonderful marriage like my parents had."

He darted a glance at her. "So what happened? How did you find out the truth?"

As the unsettling memories washed over her, she folded pleats in the hem of her dress. "Quite by accident, really. He was working on some bookkeeping, or supposedly so, in one of the offices in the back of the church. I overheard him talking on the phone." She frowned. "The old adage that eavesdroppers usually hear things they don't want to hear was certainly true in my case."

"But you listened anyway."

"Yeah," she said, her voice dripping with disgust. "From his words and his tone I could tell he was talking to a woman, one that he was *very* familiar with. Apparently she wanted him back, but Ian told her he'd found a 'little gold mine'—meaning me— and as soon as he got a ring on my finger he would be living on easy street."

"Bastard."

Dropping her head, she said quietly, "I was so stricken I couldn't think of what to call him. Then later, when we were away from the church, my anger hit me and I lashed out at him in a horrible way."

"It couldn't have been horrible enough," Cordero said grimly. His fingers tightened around the wheel. "He needed to be beaten within an inch of his life."

"No," she said with a shake of her head. "I shouldn't have been led astray. I was the one at fault. For giving in to carnal urges. For thinking that love was more important than my duty to the church."

Shocked by that remark, Cordero's gaze left the highway to stare at her. "Not hardly! You were only behaving like any normal woman. The guy was a leech. A loser. Back home we have a good remedy for men like him." He lifted his right hand from the steering wheel and made a hard fist.

It suddenly became clear to her that Cordero was a man who would always uphold his principles. He would lay his life on the line to protect the woman he loved. His outrage over Ian's behavior exposed his true ethics, and she couldn't help but admire him even more.

She said, "Well, I'm sure Ian's faced a few threatening fists in the past year or so. He's in prison now."

Stunned by this revelation, Cordero's foot unconsciously eased on the accelerator, making the car slow to a crawl. "Prison! How? Why?"

Anne-Marie's lips twisted with regret. "After our breakup he left town. In fact, he left only hours afterward. I thought he'd run because he didn't want to face Father's wrath. But that wasn't the case. A few days later, Father Granville discovered a large amount of money missing from a safe kept in the church. It was pretty obvious who took it. The police picked up Ian's trail and discovered there were several warrants out on him for fraud and other crimes. Eventually they caught him in another state and he was later convicted." She shook her head in shameful dismay. "Oh, Cordero, he'd told me he was from a nice, prominent family in South Carolina, but in reality he was a drifter with no home. With nothing really, but a sweet, deceitful line."

Long moments passed in silence and then he reached across the seat and folded her hand in his. "I'm so sorry, Anne-Marie. But you shouldn't feel ashamed because this happened to you. You made a bad choice. Everybody does from time to time. We have to forgive ourselves and move forward."

"I have forgiven myself, Cordero. But I… can't trust myself. My judgment, my purpose in life, everything was shaken after that. I guess—" she looked at him through misty eyes "—when you accused me of running and hiding, you were right. I'm afraid. It terrifies me to think of trusting another man. That's why I'll never fall in love again. I'll never get married. Focusing on my missionary work is the right thing to do. The safe thing to do."

"Is that really the way you want your life to be?" he asked softly.

She looked away from him and swallowed as tears burned in her throat. "It's the only way it can be."

Chapter Eight

For the remainder of their trip home, Cordero made a point of turning their conversation to lighter subjects. After a while he actually had Anne-Marie smiling and laughing over antics he and his brother had pulled at the ranch. But he couldn't quit thinking about the man who'd deceived her and broken her spirit.

As far as Cordero was concerned, prison was too good for someone so evil. The man's incarceration couldn't repair the damage he'd done to Anne-Marie. Cordero wasn't sure what or who could repair her, but he could now see why Jules had gone to such lengths to shake his daughter out of her doldrums.

A few minutes later, they arrived at Cane's Landing. Except for a porch light, the house was dark.

As he always did, Cordero offered her his arm as they walked to the house. This time, as they made their way through the shadows, he was acutely aware of her hand clinging to his forearm and the way her small body leaned closer than usual.

This evening had drawn them closer. He was sure of that. But did she want to be closer?

From the moment he'd first met Anne-Marie, thoughts of undressing her and making love to her had gouged him from all directions. Getting her into his bed had been a goal he'd quickly set for himself. Yet now that he'd learned about the heartache she'd endured, he wasn't at all sure about the decency of his motives.

With a mental shake of his head, Cordero silently cursed himself. Hell, since when had he ever worried about the consequences of having sex with a beautiful woman? What had come over him anyway? He wouldn't break Anne-Marie's heart. She wasn't in love with him, and he wasn't lying and making promises of marriage and babies.

Once inside, Anne-Marie crossed the room to switch on a lamp. Cordero was deeply aware of the empty spot by his side.

Turning back to him, she asked, "Would you like coffee before you go to bed?"

During the drive home, tendrils of her copper hair had escaped their pins and now curled loosely upon her shoulders. Her dusky lips were bare, her eyes sleepy. Desire struck him hard and pushed his boots across the polished floor to where she stood waiting for his answer.

"No." He curved his hands along the back of her upper arms. "Come here—to me."

"Cordero."

She said his name with a mixture of longing and regret. Focusing on that first emotion, he tugged her forward until her body brushed the front of his.

"You know that I want you," he murmured. "And I believe you want me just as much."

"I can't," she said in a choked voice.

Bending his head, he brushed his parted lips against the tender line of her neck. She shivered in his arms.

"I'm not the devil, Anne-Marie. And I'm not that bastard who's rotting away in prison. I'm just a flesh-and-blood man who wants to make love to you." His lips slipped up to her ear. His tongue gently laved the lobe before tracing a damp, tantalizing path along the outer edge. "Let me show you how it can really be."

Anne-Marie knew she should resist the sensual fog settling over her but when she opened her mouth to protest the words wouldn't come. And before she could shove them past her throat, it was too late. His lips had worked their way across her cheek and onto her lips.

The moment he kissed her, Anne-Marie felt everything inside her start to burn and melt like a lighted candle fed by a soft breeze. Her hands flattened against his chest, then slid upward until her fingers curled over his shoulders. Her lips parted and her senses reeled as his tongue glided along the roof of her mouth. A groan vibrated in her throat as she arched her body into his.

The invitation sent Cordero's hands to her bottom. He clutched the rounded curves and crushed her hips up to his. The intimate contact shot a flame straight to his loins and he knew she could feel his burgeoning desire shoving at the denim of his jeans.

With slow rocking movements, he ground her against him while his mouth made sweet, urgent love to hers. Hot blood surged in his veins and thrummed through his body like an erotic drumbeat. Her scent, her skin, the soft supple curves of her body were like sips of wine slowly and surely intoxicating his senses. The more he had, the more he wanted.

With one hand still anchoring her hips to his, the other traveled to her bodice where his fingers climbed the multitude of pleats until they touched the incredibly soft flesh above the fabric. The delicate cleavage only kindled the need to explore her breasts with his hands, his mouth.

Until then Anne-Marie had given him free rein. She'd invited rather than resisted. But the moment his fingers found the zipper at the back of her dress, she felt as if cold water had gushed from the ceiling, waking her from a trance.

Twisting her mouth from his, she used her hands to leverage her body backward and away from his.

"I—I'm sorry, Cordero. I can't—can't do this!" With a shameful groan, she whirled past him and raced up the staircase.

Cordero followed, his boots taking two stairs at a time as he tried to catch up to her. "Anne-Marie, wait! Stop!"

Ignoring his plea, she rushed into her bedroom and slammed the door just as he was about to follow her over the threshold. If he'd not been quick on his feet, the wall of wood would have smashed him in the nose. Which probably wouldn't have hurt him nearly as badly as her rejection.

Rapping his knuckles on the door, he called to her in a low voice, "Anne-Marie. Open the door. We need to talk about this."

"No, Cordero. Not tonight. Please."

Drawing in a heavy breath, he raked a hand through his hair. Everything inside him wanted to argue, to plead with her to open the door and step back into his arms.

But she obviously wasn't ready for that. And if he was ever going to have her, he wanted it to be by her inviting him all on her own. Maybe that would never happen, but any other way would be meaningless.

"Good night, Anne-Marie," he murmured to the closed door, then turned and walked to his own bedroom.

THE LATE NIGHT with Cordero caused Anne-Marie to sleep later than usual the next morning. By the time she pushed herself out of bed and got down to the kitchen for breakfast, Darcella informed her that their guest had already left for the stables.

Sipping at a cup of hot coffee, Anne-Marie leaned her hip against the cabinet. "Oh. Well, I hadn't intended to sleep so late. You should have woken me, Darcella."

The cook opened the dishwasher and placed several dirty bowls inside. "Mr. Cordero told me not to. He said you were probably tired from all the dancing you two did last night."

Darcella tossed Anne-Marie a naughty grin. "I didn't know you knew how to dance. What else are you holdin' back from me?"

Only that she'd nearly made love to their houseguest, Anne-Marie thought with despair. One more kiss and she would have given him anything and everything.

"I don't really know how to dance, Darcella. Cordero was just nice enough to guide me around the floor and keep me from falling."

The other woman chuckled. "Well, maybe you're finally going to learn what it's like to have a little fun."

Fun wasn't her lot in life. The one time she'd tried it had ended in painful shame. Frowning, Anne-Marie grabbed a plate from the cabinet and went over to the stove where Darcella had left scrambled eggs and biscuits in a warmer.

"Darcella, don't start thinking this is going to change things. I'm not a fun girl."

Turning away from the double sink, Darcella folded her arms across her breasts as she studied Anne-Marie. "Humph. Like you needed to remind me of that," she said with something close to a snort. "If you get the tiniest smile on your face you feel guilty. If you laugh you think someone ought to put you in chains. When are you ever going to forgive yourself, Anne-Marie?"

Anne-Marie's shoulders slumped as she ladled food onto her plate. "Darcella, now is not the time to start in on me about—"

"Now is the perfect time," Darcella interrupted with unusual temper. "Mr. Cordero will only be here for a few days. If you don't make the most of his company then— well, then you're not nearly the woman your mother was."

Her lips set in a grim, silent line, Anne-Marie marched outside and took a seat on the side porch to eat her breakfast. But the eggs and biscuits were tasteless as she chewed. She didn't know why Darcella had made such a heartless remark. Especially when it had always been obvious to Anne-Marie, and most everyone else, that she could never hold a light to Fiona Duveuil. Had it been necessary for the cook to remind her?

Fiona had been beautiful and intelligent, compassionate and full of life. She'd chosen a good, loving man for a husband and had given him a child, even as she had served the church and others who'd been in need.

She'd done everything right—except dying and leaving Anne-Marie without a mother.

Trying not to dwell on that sober memory, Anne-Marie finished the food on her plate and was about to go back into the house when Darcella appeared with a portable phone in her hand.

"It's Miss Audra." Her expression distant, Darcella handed the receiver to Anne-Marie then turned and went back into the house.

Sighing, Anne-Marie put the phone to her ear. "Hello, cousin."

"Hello, yourself. Sorry for interrupting your breakfast, but I couldn't wait any longer. I wanted to know how your night on the town went."

Anne-Marie closed her eyes. Darcella and Audra were behaving as though Anne-Marie had never gone on a date in her life. Which was ridiculous. As a teenager, she'd dated on several occasions. She'd even enjoyed male companionship. Yet she'd always had her heart set on devoting her life to her faith. Until Ian, she thought bitterly. And after him, even a casual date had felt repulsive to her. But now, with Cordero, she was feeling things, thinking things, she never had before. She could only wonder if something inside her was collapsing or merely waking up.

"It was very nice."

Audra let out an impatient huff. "That's all? Just nice? Can't you tell me more?"

Leaning back in her chair, Anne-Marie absently combed her fingers through her hair. "Audra, believe me, it couldn't compare to one of *your* dates. But we had a lovely supper at a little place on Bourbon Street and then Cordero surprised me by taking me to a warehouse where a live band played zydeco and Cajun music."

"Don't tell me you danced!" Audra exclaimed.

A dreamy smile lifted the corners of Anne-Marie's lips. "Several times. I was surprised that it came back to me. I didn't step on his toes even once."

"Lord, lord, am I out of bed or am I still dreaming?" Audra teased. "And how could dancing come back to you when you sat through your whole senior prom?"

Anne-Marie had to laugh. How could she not when the day was sunny and bright and Cordero was still here on the plantation?

Somehow just knowing he was close made each minute special.

"Well, it did. And I enjoyed myself, Audra. I really did. Cordero is—well, special."

"Now you're making some sense," Audra said with approval. "So now what? Does the man seem interested—I mean, romantically?"

Even though Audra was miles away, her question was enough to color Anne-Marie's face with embarrassed heat. There was no way her cousin could know that she'd come close to giving in to Cordero's kisses and inviting him up to her bedroom.

Her sigh was unconsciously wistful. "Audra, the man is interested. But not romantically. He, uh, he's not looking for long-term with any woman. And since we live hundreds of miles apart, he certainly isn't going to be looking at me in that light."

"Oh. But you say he *is* interested. That must mean sex. Is that what you're trying to tell me? The man wants to get you into his bed?"

Leave it to Audra to blurt out the obvious, Anne-Marie thought drily. "That pretty much sums it up."

Audra released a wicked little laugh. "Honey, that's a great start. The love part will come later."

"Audra!" Anne-Marie primly scolded. "I'm not looking for the love part or any part from Cordero."

Her voice suddenly going serious, Audra retorted, "Really, Anne-Marie? Are you being honest with me? Because I don't think so. I saw the way you looked at him. You had a light in your eyes that I'd never seen before. Maybe you'd better think long and hard before you dismiss your feelings."

Anne-Marie had never heard her cousin talk so seriously before and the idea shook her.

"I'll think, Audra," she promised. "Right now I've got to get off the phone. We'll talk later."

She pushed the button to disconnect the call, then finished the last of her cooling coffee. When she carried her dirty dishes back into the house, Darcella was sitting on a step stool at the end of a butcher block. She was pinching the heads off a pile of fresh shrimp and throwing the bodies into a colander. Her movements were automatic and Anne-Marie could see she had other things on her mind.

"Is everything okay with Miss Audra?" Darcella asked.

Anne-Marie placed her dirty dishes in the dishwasher. "Yes. She's fine." Turning back to the cook, she looked pointedly at the stool. "Is something wrong? You don't normally sit when you're working here in the kitchen."

Darcella shook her head. "Nothing that a little rest won't cure. I twisted my ankle last night when I climbed the steps to my house."

Concerned now, Anne-Marie kneeled down to inspect the injury. Darcella's right ankle was markedly swollen and blue around the bone. She felt terrible for not noticing it in the first place.

"Darcella! Why did you even come to work like this? You need to get to the doctor. I'm sure he'll order you off your feet. In fact, I'm not waiting on the doctor! I'm ordering you off work as of now. I'll put this stuff away and then I'll drive you home."

Darcella grimaced. "Can't do that. Not when there's company to feed."

"Forget Cordero," Anne-Marie told her. "He doesn't expect gourmet meals three times a day. And he surely wouldn't want you working in pain. Besides, I'll take care of him." Rising to her full height, she placed an arm around Darcella's shoulders and squeezed. "I'm sorry if I seemed short earlier. I guess I'm a little sensitive where Cordero is concerned."

Darcella grinned. "Maybe because you like him—a lot. Don't you think?"

Dropping her head, Anne-Marie nodded. "Yes. I do like him—very much. More than I've ever liked any man."

Smoothing a hand over Anne-Marie's hair, Darcella said with regret, "I'm the one who should be apologizing. I shouldn't have said that to you—about your mother." She sighed. "But Miss Fiona wanted you to have all the things that she had. She wanted you to grow up and marry a fine man, have babies and know what it was like to be loved and wanted. There's no sin in that, Anne-Marie. No sin at all."

A hot lump of tears collected in Anne-

Marie's throat, forcing her to swallow several times before she was finally able to speak.

"Yes, I know," she said in a choked voice. Clearing her throat, she took Darcella by the hand and urged her up from the seat. "Come on. Let's get your things and I'll drive you home. We'll call the doctor from there."

Anne-Marie helped the cook, then quickly put the shrimp away in the refrigerator. Before they left, she dashed off a note to Cordero and placed the piece of paper on the cabinet counter where he would likely come for a clean glass.

A half hour later, when she returned to Cane's Landing, Cordero was nowhere about and she wondered if he was expecting her to show up at the stables for another ride. After all, getting her reacquainted with riding was the reason he was here, she reminded herself. But after last night, after kissing him so wantonly, that idea seemed ludicrous. He wasn't teaching her about horses, he was teaching her about love.

The notion that she could be falling in love with Cordero hit her like a ton of bricks. She sank into a chair at the kitchen table and buried her face in her hands.

Last night she'd raced to her bedroom and refused to speak to Cordero because she'd been afraid. Not of him. But of herself. She'd known, even before she'd turned to putty in his arms, that he was settling in her heart like a glowing ember. She couldn't douse it. She couldn't ignore it. So she'd run, believing that if she didn't give in to him or herself, she could keep her heart safe.

But she wasn't safe. She still wanted him. She still needed to see his smile, hear his voice, feel his arms around her. Yet he didn't want her love. He only wanted her body.

Honey, that's a great start. The love part will come later.

Would it? The only thing she knew for sure was that running would never give her the answer.

An hour later, she'd packed a lunch of cold sandwiches in a small basket, changed into black Capri pants and a skinny tank top, then headed to the stables.

When she approached the long string of wooden structures she spotted Cordero sitting with Ben in the shade of a cypress tree. Ben was laughing, something she'd not seen him do in a long time and the sight momentarily lifted her heart. Cordero had touched everyone at Cane's Landing and brought a smile to their faces. That could only be good.

"Well now," Ben said teasingly as he caught sight of Anne-Marie, "here comes Miss Anne-Marie. You finally decided to rise and shine?"

She walked over to the two men who were using overturned feed buckets for seats. "I've been up for a long while. I've been busy. I had to take Darcella home."

Cordero looked at her with concern. "Is something wrong?"

"She twisted her ankle last night and it's blue and swollen. I made a doctor's appointment for her later this afternoon. She's going to have a friend drive her."

Ben snorted. "The woman shouldn't have come in to work in the first place. She knows I can take over kitchen duties if need be."

Anne-Marie glanced over at Cordero and gave him a conspiring wink. "That's what she was worried about. She said Ben's biscuits taste like gun waddin'—whatever that is."

A look of outrage passed over the caretaker's face. "Why, that old biddy! I'll tell you what it is. It's a rag used to shove a bullet down the barrel of a musket. It's black and oily and—"

He broke off as Anne-Marie began to giggle. "Oh, Ben, Darcella didn't say any of that. I'm just teasing you."

Reaching over, she patted the old man's shoulder as she said to Cordero, "Ben's cooking is really quite good. Course Father and I can't rave too much about it or Darcella will get jealous." To Ben she said, "Thank you for offering to take over the kitchen duties, Ben, but there's plenty in the refrigerator for Cordero and I to eat."

Grinning now, Ben pointed to the basket hanging from her right hand. "What's that? You bring the horses some apples?"

"No." Feeling a little embarrassed now, she glanced at Cordero, who was watching her with raised eyebrows. "Actually it's a picnic lunch for Cordero—and me."

"Oh." Ben tossed a sly wink at Cordero.

"Sounds like we'd better get the horses saddled again, son."

"Uh, no," Anne-Marie quickly replied. "I thought Cordero might like to take a boat trip down the river."

Totally surprised now, Ben exclaimed, "You mean in that old rowboat?"

She frowned at Ben. "Well, why not? Cordero's a big, strong man. He can row. And it's a beautiful day for it." She turned a questioning eye on Cordero. "Would you like to go?"

To say Cordero was taken aback by her invitation would be putting it mildly. For most of the morning, he'd been hanging around the stables trying to find the nerve to face her, to apologize for his forward behavior. He'd expected her to be as frosty as a December morning, but instead she was laughing and playful and inviting him on a picnic. He wasn't going to stop and wonder about the change in her. He was simply going to enjoy it.

"Sure." He rose to his feet. "Where is this boat you're talking about?"

She pointed toward the woods at the back of the stables. "There's a dim trail down to the river over there. Father keeps the boat tied at a dock."

He looked down at Ben. "I hate to leave good company, Ben, but when a woman calls there's not much else a man can do."

Anne-Marie looked down at the basket she was carrying. "I have plenty of sandwiches, Ben, if you'd like one."

He waved the two of them in the direction of the river. "I got my lunch in the tack room. You two go on and be safe. I'll be right here if you need me."

Taking the basket from Anne-Marie, he curled his free hand around her upper arm. As they walked across a grassy slope, he said, "This is a very nice surprise. I was just about to come back to the house to see if you wanted to ride."

Darting a glance up at him, she said, "If you'd rather ride, we can. I just thought—it might be nice to go down the river."

As Cordero looked down at her, he was surprised at how beautiful she looked to him today, even more than she had last night in her sexy red dress. Which didn't make a lot of sense. Today she was dressed casually and her hair was flowing loose upon her shoulders. Yet it was not her clothing or her hair that made her appearance different. It was something he couldn't quite define. A glowing aura about her face that made her eyes look like jewels and her lips look like velvet rose petals.

He was spellbound, and the scary part about it was that he knew it.

"We can ride later. I'd love to see the river."

A smile radiated across her face. "Good. And if you're worrying about rowing, don't. I'm good at it. I'll help you."

The only thing Cordero was worried about was keeping his hands off her. But then maybe she'd had a change of heart. Could it be that she'd decided making love to him wasn't the evil thing she'd first thought it to be?

Cordero could only wonder and wait and try to not to dwell on how important this woman had become to him.

Chapter Nine

The boat turned out to be a long wooden structure with a V-shaped bow and deep sides. Three wooden benches crossed the midsection of the structure. A pair of long wooden oars were on the floor, along with a couple of orange life jackets.

Anne-Marie took a seat on the middle bench and Cordero untied the mooring ropes then took a seat beside her.

Picking up one of the oars, he dipped it in the water and pushed them away from the small wooden dock. "Bear with me, Anne-

Marie. I haven't done this sort of thing in a long, long time."

The river was a dark, murky green and smooth as glass. One push of the oar sent the boat gliding for several feet.

"Do you have a river on your ranch?" she asked.

He nodded. "The San Antonio. But you never know how you're going to find it. Sometimes it's wild and flooding its banks. Other times there are only spotty holes of water. The climate back home can be extreme."

Along the riverbanks, willows, cypress and pine grew tall and thick. Limbs bowed over the water, leaves dipped their fingers and blocked out the overhead sun. At the river's edge, water hibiscus bloomed purple while bright green duckweed created a green carpet on the surface. Far ahead of them, birds swooped and dragonflies darted from their path.

It was a beautiful scene, but Cordero could hardly focus on his surroundings. Not when the delicate scent of flowers emanated from Anne-Marie's skin and the warmth of her shoulder and thigh spun his mind back to last night and the feel of her body sliding against his.

Like a haunting melody, she was taking over his thoughts. He wasn't at all sure that was a healthy thing for a man who liked his freedom. Trying to shake that dour notion from his mind, he spoke the first question that came to him. "Are there gators in this river?"

"Sure. Plenty of them," she answered. "They mostly surface in the summer months. We've never had one attack the boat, though. Have you seen one before?"

He laughed. "They're thick where I come from. And they're big. Very big."

She chuckled. "I should have seen that coming. Everything is bigger in the Lone Star State, right?"

He laughed with her. "I don't know about that. But my brother, Matt, nearly lost his leg to a gator when we were kids. We were in one of the back pastures swimming, instead of hunting calves like Dad had told us to do. The river was up from heavy rains and the current always washes the alligators and snakes out of their homes."

"How did your brother get away?"

"I hit the alligator over the head with a stick. That distracted the thing long enough for Matt to get away."

"So how did you get away?" she wanted to know.

Sunlight emerged from the overhanging branches above them and momentarily lit her face. His eyes followed the sun's glow and he was amazed all over again at the smoothness of her pearly skin and the fieriness of her hair.

A grin tilted one corner of his lips. "Swam as fast as I could and prayed."

She smiled and then with a wistful sigh, she looped her arm through his and rested her head against his shoulder. "I'm glad you came to Cane's Landing, Cordero."

He paused his rowing and looked down at her. "Do you really mean that?"

"You sound doubtful."

"Well, you weren't too happy with your father that first night. It was pretty obvious you wanted me gone."

Pink color appeared on her cheeks. "I don't like being manipulated. And as for you, I didn't know you."

A corner of his mouth pulled into a grin. "And you do now?"

She turned her gaze up the river as her fingers moved up and down his forearm. "Well, I don't know everything about you. But I'm learning."

He swallowed. "How far did you want to go? Down the river, I mean."

"I thought we'd go as far as the landing and eat our lunch there. Why, are you getting tired?"

Her question very nearly made him laugh. He could row for hours as long as she sat next to him, touching him as though he were something precious. She filled him with energy. And something else that he couldn't define or understand. He only knew that the feeling was thrilling.

"No. Besides, we're not in any hurry, are we?"

"Not at all."

TWENTY MINUTES LATER, the old wooden landing appeared. In bygone days, boats had docked and waited there to be loaded with cane that had been cut by hand and pulled to the river by mules and wagons. Over time, the planks had rotted, but Jules had hired workmen to restore the piers and the flooring. Now carpenters came out yearly to make sure the landing was maintained.

Cordero moored the boat alongside the long dock, then helped Anne-Marie climb up. After he fetched the picnic basket, he joined her on the wooden floor.

"Are we going to eat here on the dock?" he asked.

"No. Let's find shade where it will be cooler."

He chuckled. "And swat mosquitoes while we eat?"

She shot him a comical frown. "An outdoor man like you worrying about a few tiny bugs?" She shook her head. "If you can't take it, I put a bottle of repellent in the lunch basket."

He laughed. "I was only kidding." He gestured toward the bank. "You lead the way and I'll follow."

Anne-Marie explored the nearby area until she found a spot at the edge of the water where the undergrowth was short and the shade from a willow was deep and cool.

"Sorry I didn't bring a tablecloth," she said as they both sank down to the ground. "I wanted to travel light."

"The ground is a cowboy's pallet, Anne-Marie. This is where I feel comfortable."

Using the fat trunk of the willow for a backrest, he stretched out his long legs and crossed his boots at the ankles. Anne-Marie sat at his side with her legs underneath her and quickly doled out the contents of the basket.

For several moments they ate and made small talk, but once he'd eaten a piece of cake and brushed the crumbs from his hands, he looked at her with a frankness that made her cheeks burn.

"You know you've surprised me, don't you?"

Anne-Marie crumpled the empty plastic wrap in her hand and shoved it back into the basket. "How do you mean?" she asked carefully.

"I mean, last night. You weren't exactly happy with me. Now today, I think you're actually enjoying being with me."

Being with him had always been a joy. Or at least that was how it felt to Anne-Marie. Somehow his warmth and laughter, the depth of his kisses, had opened her eyes and her heart and she was seeing the world— him—in a whole new way.

Glancing at him through lowered lashes, she said, "If you think I was angry with you last night, Cordero, you're wrong. I was more annoyed with myself—and I guess I was running scared. Just like you said."

His expression earnest, he leaned toward her. "Why?"

Her gaze roamed his face until it finally settled on the hewed line of his lips. "Because I knew if I didn't run, I was going to end up making love to you."

A faint groan rumbled in his throat. "And what about now?"

Her heart began to beat with wild, sweet anticipation. She drew in a deep breath, as though readying herself to jump into the deepest end of the pool. "I'm tired of running, Cordero. I'm tired of shutting myself away from life—from you."

Scooting closer, she lifted the black Stetson from his head. After placing it out of the way, she gently framed his face with her hands.

"I want you," she whispered. "I don't know any other way to say it."

He swallowed hard as his eyes searched hers. Then his head bent until his forehead touched hers. "My sweet, Anne-Marie," he murmured. "Do you know what you're saying?"

Slipping her arms around his neck, Anne-Marie pressed her lips to his. "Don't keep asking questions, cowboy."

Happy to follow her orders, his lips captured hers in a kiss that was even hungrier than those of the night before. The connection caused Anne-Marie's head to fall into the curve of his arm and her body to twist until she was partially lying across his lap. Cordero's hands slid across her back then crawled beneath the hem of her tank top.

His fingers were warm and gritty against her skin as they slowly slid along her rib cage, then moved up and up until they met the lacy fabric of her bra. Not to be deterred, he released the single snap between her breasts. The plump mounds were bared to the exploration of his hands.

Fire ripped through her as his forefinger traced a lazy circle around each nipple and she groaned with a need that was as raw and primal as the deep woods surrounding them. Breaking the contact of their lips, he spattered kisses across her cheeks, down her throat and along her shoulders while his hands kneaded her breasts, formed them to the shape of his palms.

"Anne-Marie. Anne-Marie," he whispered huskily. "I've never felt anything like this. I've never wanted like this."

Beyond her closed eyes, bright green and blue checkered together, spinning like a brilliant star. Inside of her, a fire burned, working its way upward, eating at the cold shell she'd once cocooned herself in.

"Neither…have I," she said in a strained, helpless tone.

His hands left her breasts to gather the hem of her top. Instinctively, she held up her arms and waited for him to pull the piece of clothing over her head.

"Is anyone ever around here?" he asked huskily, as he pushed the straps of her bra over her shoulders and down her arms.

Anne-Marie shivered as much from his heated gaze as from the touch of his fingers along her delicate skin.

"No. No one comes around here except for me or my father. And we know where he is."

"That's good. I don't want to worry about someone coming up on us." His hands dipped into the thick red waves falling onto her shoulders. "I want to focus my whole attention on you."

The soft growl in his voice was even sexier than the glint in his eyes and Anne-Marie was amazed that she'd been able to resist him for this long.

"I'm yours, Cordero," she whispered. "Totally yours."

She was surprised to see a humbled expression steal over his face, but she didn't have time to ponder his reaction. His head suddenly dipped and his mouth latched on to one rosy nipple.

Like streaks of lightning, desire sizzled through her, jolting her with the impact. Crying out, she dug her fingers into his hair and arched her upper body toward the tender suckling.

On and on, he tasted, nibbled, tugged at her breasts until she could no longer bear the heat building between the juncture of her thighs. She wanted him. So desperately.

She was twisting against him, trying to unfasten the buttons of his shirt, when he finally pulled away from her. She gazed at his face through a glaze of raw desire.

"This isn't the place to make love to you, Anne-Marie," he said with undisguised agony. "I want it to be right—special."

Stunned by his words, she wrapped her arms around his neck and buried her face in the curve of his shoulder. "This is special, Cordero. I have always loved this place. I used to come here with my mother and we would sit and talk about our hopes and dreams." Lifting her head, she looked into his eyes and smiled. "What is that old cowboy motto? The ground for your bed, the stars for your blanket. Show me what it means, Cordero."

"Oh, my darling. My sweet Anne-Marie," he whispered, "I don't deserve you. Or this. But I'm not strong enough to get up and walk away. Don't hate me later. Promise me."

A rough lump of emotion gathered in

her throat, making it almost impossible to speak. "I could never hate you, my love."

She reached for the buttons on his shirt again and her fingers fumbled until the last one was dealt with. When she finally pushed the fabric apart, he pulled the garment from his shoulders and spread it over the grass behind them.

The gesture brought tears to her eyes, but she hid them as he laid her down on the makeshift bed and quickly removed the rest of her clothing. Once he had them tossed aside, she opened her eyes to see him stand and deal with his own jeans and boots.

As Anne-Marie watched, her breath caught in her throat. He was solid, sculpted muscle and his arousal couldn't have been more evident.

She forced herself to breathe as he kneeled over her and then air passed her lips as a yearning sigh when he slid his arms beneath her and lifted her upper body next to his.

Slow minutes ticked by as he kissed her, touched her, explored every gentle curve. Beneath him Anne-Marie's head danced in a merry circle, singing like a joyous choir.

Her hands kneaded the muscles on his back. Her fingers skipped and jumped down the vertebrae of his spine until she flattened her palms against his buttocks and urged him to join them together.

"I don't have any protection," he mouthed against her damp forehead.

She paused, but only for a second. "I— don't, either. But it—doesn't matter."

He groaned with a hunger that had nothing to do with his body and everything to do with his heart. He was gripped with an urgency that superseded everything. "No. I guess not. Because I sure as hell can't get up and leave you now."

Nor could she let him. Opening her legs, she urged him to unite their bodies and make them one.

Cordero didn't hesitate. He couldn't. Hot blood pounded inside his head. His loins ached to the point of exploding. Nothing would assuage his pain except burying himself in her softness.

When he entered her he tried to go slowly and give her time to adjust. Yet the need to drive himself into her was fierce. So fierce that sweat poured from his forehead and forced him to grit his teeth.

But suddenly Anne-Marie solved his problem by arching her hips, sheathing him with delicious heat. The sudden rush of pleasure splintered through him like lightning splitting the clouds and striking the earth. Her legs were bands of silk wrapping around him tighter and tighter. Her hands flattened against the back of his thighs, urging him closer, deeper.

Cordero had never made love to a woman without the protection of a condom. The fact left him feeling strangely vulnerable, yet sweetly connected to Anne-Marie in a way he'd never experienced. And the sensation of flesh against flesh was only a part of the pleasure playing with his emotions. He was naked and exposed, giving her and showing her the real him.

He could feel her slender body writhing, twisting against his. Her hands were on his back, his legs and buttocks, skating across his sweaty skin as though she couldn't get enough of touching him.

She was all goodness and sweetness and as Cordero drove himself into her, for the first time in his life, he wanted to be a part of someone else. He wanted that goodness to flow into him, to fill him up, even to the center of his heart. He wanted to take that part of her with him. Forever and ever.

Anne-Marie was certain the earth beneath her tilted, tossing her toward heaven. Crying out, she clung to his shoulders. Willow leaves and blue sky blurred together until nothing but bright stars rained down on her, pricking her with rays of golden light. Above her, Cordero made a guttural sound of release and clutched her to him as though she was his anchor on a storm-tossed sea.

Long moments passed before Cordero rolled his weight off her body. Then he stretched on his side to look down at her face.

"You're sweating," he said.

She smiled drowsily. "I wonder why," she murmured wryly. Opening her eyes, she looked up into his handsome face. Emotions squeezed inside her chest, filled her heart with pleasure and pain.

His forefinger pressed into the middle of

her lower lip. "The day is hot. And I've got just the remedy."

"I thought you just did."

Chuckles gurgled in his throat. "Oh, you naughty girl. You haven't seen the half of it yet."

Before she could question that remark he rose to his feet, pulling her along with him.

"Cordero! What—" She squealed as he lifted her in his arms and moved away from the shelter of the willow. "Where are we going? My clothes—"

"You won't need them," he interrupted.

Before she realized what he was up to, he stopped at the edge of the dock and dropped her into the water.

She came up sputtering and yelling as she wiped at strands of hair stuck to her face. "Cordero! There are alligators in here!"

"Don't worry, darlin' I'd never let them get you."

He jumped in beside her and the force of the waves sucked her beneath the water with him. Their arms and legs tangled and then he wrapped her against him and kicked the weight of their bodies toward the surface.

They were both laughing as their heads

broke through the rippling waves. Using one hand to tread water, he used the other to push the hair from Anne-Marie's face. Once it was tucked behind her ears he kissed the droplets from her cheeks.

"Cool now?" he asked, his white teeth gleaming as he grinned at her.

The buoyancy of the water thrust their bodies together and Anne-Marie used the weightlessness to wrap her legs around Cordero's waist.

"Not yet."

He brought his lips next to hers. "I thought you were worried about alligators."

She circled her arms around his neck. "Not when I have you here to keep me safe."

LATE EVENING SENT long shadows across the yard when they finally returned to the house. While Cordero went upstairs to shower, Anne-Marie fed Lucy on the back porch, then checked the answering machine.

Darcella had left a message saying the doctor had ordered her off her feet for the next few days. Anne-Marie called her to make sure she was following his orders, then made a quick call to her father. Jules sounded extremely chipper for a man sitting in a hospital room. Especially when Anne-Marie told him that she and Cordero had taken a boat ride down to the landing. As she hung up the phone it dawned on her that Jules had not only purchased the horses for her sake, he'd brought Cordero to Cane's Landing for her sake, too.

The realization should have angered her, even humiliated her, but now it only brought a wry smile to her face. After all, how could she be angry when she felt her heart, her mind, her whole body glowing.

After a shower and a change of clothes, Anne-Marie went back to the kitchen and began to pull food from the refrigerator. By the time Cordero appeared, she'd set the table on the side porch and carried out a plate of roast chicken, along with bowls of potato salad, cheese and fruit.

"Have a seat, Mr. Sanchez. Your supper is ready."

Walking up behind her, he slipped his arms around her waist and pressed his lips to the top of her hair. She smelled like a creamy magnolia blossom and he simply drew in the scent of her and let the warmth of her body seep into his.

"I didn't realize you were this handy in the kitchen," he said teasingly.

"I have to confess. Darcella already had the chicken and potato salad prepared. But, I *can* cook. After Mama died I spent a lot of time with Darcella. Being with her comforted me. And along the way I picked up a little knowledge about the kitchen."

He squeezed her shoulder in an understanding way, then reached to pull out a chair from the table.

"Have a seat, my lady."

He joined her after he'd pulled a chair close to hers.

"Darcella left a phone message while we were gone. The doctor has ordered her to rest her ankle the next few days. I called her and told her that we'd be fine."

"That's good."

"I also called Father. He's doing fine," she said happily. "He was pleased to hear we'd spent the day together."

She handed him the platter of chicken and he speared several slices onto his plate. "I'm glad. Your father is a good man. He loves you very much."

Anne-Marie paused from filling her own plate to look thoughtfully at him. "Cordero, I think Father invited you here to Cane's Landing solely for my sake. Is that true?"

Surprise lifted his brows and then his expression turned sheepish. "No. I mean, actually I came here to deliver the horses. But—I think Jules did a little calculating on his own. Don't get angry when I tell you this, Anne-Marie, but your father didn't really have a spell with his heart. He ordered the doctor to put him in the hospital and threatened to take away his financial donations to the hospital if he didn't. I didn't learn about this until after I arrived and we visited Jules in the hospital."

Shaking her head with dismay, Anne-Marie didn't know whether to be angry, insulted or happy. "I should have guessed," she said finally. "It was plain that he was manipulating us, but I didn't realize he'd gone to such lengths." She sighed. "At least I know now that his heart is okay. I guess that's the most important thing."

Cordero slipped his hand over hers.

"That. And the fact that he brought us to-gether."

But their time was limited. The thought pierced her with such sudden pain that she quickly brushed it away as she would a stinging wasp.

She couldn't think about Cordero climb-ing into his truck and leaving for Texas. That would come later. Right now they had the night ahead of them and all she wanted to do was give him her love.

Chapter Ten

When Cordero woke the next morning, the sun was already shining and the spot beside him was empty. Glancing at the footboard of the bed, he saw that Anne-Marie's clothes were gone and he could only guess that she was in the shower or down in the kitchen preparing breakfast.

Raking a hand through his tousled hair, he turned on his side and gazed at the space where she'd lain beside him throughout the night. The fragile scent of her still lingered on the sheets and that was all it took to fill his mind with her image. Her lovely face and creamy skin, her rosy nipples peeking through strands of fiery red hair, her warm giving body treating him with delights that had jolted and shaken him to the very core of his being.

He'd never felt like this before and the idea that he was changing—that for the first time in his life he needed a woman, one woman—was enough to put him in a panic.

Being here with Anne-Marie was like being in paradise. He wanted to stay until this obsessive need for her wore itself out. But another part of him argued that to stay longer would only make him fall deeper into the tender web she was weaving around him.

The cell phone that he'd left on the bedside table suddenly rang and he stared at it in surprise. He only used this particular phone for family and none of them would call unless it was absolutely necessary.

Fearing something had happened, he snatched it up. "Cordero here."

"Cordero. I'm sorry to interrupt your vacation. Do you have a moment to talk?"

The sound of his sister-in-law's voice

took him aback. He'd been expecting Matt or Lex.

"Juliet? What's wrong?" he asked without preamble.

"Nothing. I'm sorry if I've worried you. It's nothing like an emergency. I'm actually calling because your brother refused to."

"Matt? Where is he?"

She let out a weary sigh that told him things at the Sandbur must be hectic.

"He's already left the house this morning. A cattle buyer is coming to look at a bull. And then he's got to meet with some man about the auction."

For several months now his brother, Matt, had been planning a live television auction from the Sandbur. Buyers would be present at the ranch, along with bids taken over the phone by viewers in other states. The event required a lot of Matt's time and energy, not to mention taking away from other tasks that needed his attention.

"Is Matt okay?" Cordero asked.

"Yes. He's fine—just tired. The reason I'm calling is to see how much longer you'll be staying there in Louisiana."

He could hear a hesitant tone in her voice

as though she didn't want to get to the real point.

"Why?" Cordero asked. "Why didn't he want to call me?"

"Because he didn't want to bother you. But I thought you should know that a few of the horses have come down with shipping fever. We don't know how they got it. Matt thinks they were contaminated when one of the wranglers hauled them to the vet for vaccinations. Anyway, your father has been trying to take extra care of them and he refuses to let the wranglers help. He's wearing himself out and—"

"I need to be there. He'll trust me to do what's needed," he finished before Juliet could. "And when I do get there I'm going to argue my case to Matt and Lex about the need to hire a resident vet on the Sandbur."

"For whatever it's worth, I'll back you up on that, Cordero. I'm just sorry to bother you with all this. But I thought you'd want to know about the situation."

"I do. I'm glad you called." Glancing toward the ceiling he blew out a long breath. What was Anne-Marie going to think? And how could he bear to tell her goodbye? "I'll start home today."

"Are you sure? I mean, this isn't exactly an emergency. And you're on vacation. I just wanted you to be aware of what was going on. Matt keeps insisting he can handle it."

"Yeah, sure. Matt has his hands full and then some. Don't worry about it, Juliet. I've had several days off already. It's time I come home." And time he remembered where his heart was supposed to be, he thought glumly.

He ended the conversation and had just put the cell phone away when Anne-Marie knocked lightly on the door and entered carrying a tray of coffee.

She wore a yellow sundress and her long hair was gathered into a ponytail behind one ear. The sight of her was like the appearance of a daffodil after a long, hard winter.

Scooting up in the bed, he propped himself against the headboard and grinned to cover the unsettled feelings swirling around inside him. "What is this? Darcella didn't do this for me."

"She'd better not have," she teased. "Seeing you naked in bed would have sent her into a faint."

"Hmm. You seem to be dealing with it quite well," he said with amusement.

She placed the tray on the nightstand, then took a seat on the edge of the mattress as she filled the cup with steaming coffee. Watching her, Cordero let his mind wander back through the night, remembering the way it had felt to make love to her, to drift off to sleep with her body draped over his.

"That's because I've gotten over the shock."

She handed him the coffee, then leaned her head close enough to plant a soft kiss on his lips.

The tempting touch brought Cordero's hand up to the back of her head. For long moments he held her lips to his and feasted on the sweet, honeyed taste of her mouth.

"That was a very nice good morning," she murmured once he finally released her.

He lifted the cup to his lips. After a careful sip, he studied her over the rim. "I'll admit I've never woken to a prettier sight."

He'd meant the words to come out·on a

light note; instead his throat had suddenly constricted, making them a raspy murmur.

"Flattery," she softly accused.

Her eyes filled with shyness and something else that pierced his chest and forced him to drop his gaze. The urge to set aside the coffee and reach for her was so great that the muscles in his stomach clenched. Yet he couldn't follow the urges rushing through him. Now that he had to leave, it wouldn't be right. He couldn't take her into his arms and peel the yellow dress from her body. He couldn't make love to her. Not now. Not ever again.

Oh, God, why was he feeling this way? He prayed for the answer. This awful ache inside him wasn't supposed to be part of the deal. He was supposed feel happy about kissing her goodbye and riding off into the sunset. That was the way a cowboy kept his freedom.

"Uh, have you been up long?" he finally asked.

"Long enough to fix breakfast. Are you hungry?"

Only for her, he thought. But he'd get over the craving. He had to.

"Sure. I'm always hungry. Just let me get a quick shower and I'll be right down," he told her.

She leaned over and kissed him lightly on the cheek, then eased off the bed. "I'll go put everything on the table," she said and headed out of the room.

As soon as the door shut behind her, Cordero swung his feet to the floor and headed to the shower. Hopefully a burst of cold water would clear his head enough so he could see his way back to Texas.

SOMETHING WAS WRONG. Anne-Marie had sensed it when she'd taken coffee to his room and kissed him. A part of him had seemed to be in another place. And now that the two of them were finishing the last bites of breakfast, she could see he was preoccupied.

Placing her coffee cup back on its saucer, she dabbed a napkin to her lips. "Cordero—"

"I need—"

Their words came out together, tangled, then halted in awkward silence.

Finally, Anne-Marie gave him a palms-up gesture. "You first," she insisted.

His face sober, he leaned back in his chair. "I was only going to say that I need to talk to you." He glanced at her, then rose to his feet and held a hand down to her. "Let's go outside. To the garden."

Anne-Marie's heart thudded with dread as they walked around the porch and down the steps to Fiona's rose garden. Whatever was on his mind couldn't be good, she thought, and she tried to prepare herself for what was about to come.

As they'd eaten breakfast, clouds had rolled in from the south, blotting out the morning sun and blanketing the plantation with humid heat. Nothing was stirring in the garden. Not even the birds or squirrels. And Anne-Marie wondered if the little creatures were hiding in anticipation of an oncoming storm.

Once they reached the wrought-iron bench that faced the cherub fountain, Cordero suggested they sit. Anne-Marie sank onto the seat and waited until he eased down beside her before she turned her knees toward him.

"I've never seen you looking so serious, Cordero. Has something happened with your family?"

He looked at her, then turned his head away and wiped a hand over his face. "I got a call from my sister-in-law. A few of the horses have shipping fever."

"Is this something serious?"

Nodding, he said, "It's like a bad flu and very contagious."

"Oh. I'm so sorry."

Yes, that would be just like Anne-Marie, he thought. She would always think of others, even animals, before herself.

"Yeah, I wish all of this hadn't happened. Juliet says that Dad is working way too many hours trying to take care of the horses. He's the sort that won't trust just anyone to deal with his babies."

"Except you."

She was perceptive. Maybe too much so, because at this moment he wasn't doing a very good job of hiding the agony he was feeling about leaving her.

"Yeah. How did you guess?"

She shrugged one shoulder. "I didn't have to guess. Horses aren't just livestock.

They're friends and companions. Your father doesn't trust their welfare to just anyone."

Releasing a rough breath, he reached for her hands. "I should have known you would understand."

Anne-Marie watched his mouth twist with regret and she realized he was trying to tell her goodbye. The word was like a stone dropping to the bottom of her heart, weighing it down with a sadness such as she'd never experienced before.

Her throat grew thicker and thicker until she had to swallow before she could speak. "Yes," she said quietly. "I understand that you have to go home. Your father needs you."

He looked away from her and she closed her eyes as his fingertips made smooth circles against the back of her hand.

"Normally it wouldn't be that way," he said. "But Matt is getting things ready for a televised cattle auction. And Dad isn't a spring chicken anymore—especially after all he's been through."

What could she say? Think? After all, she'd known this time would come, that his visit here to Cane's Landing would eventually end. Only she'd believed she would have more time with him, at least until the end of the week. Maybe a tiny part of her had hoped their lovemaking had affected him as much as it had her. Maybe she'd been unconsciously envisioning him telling her that he'd fallen in love with her, that he couldn't live without her. But that was only the dream of a foolish woman. Cordero wasn't the loving, marrying kind.

"So you have to leave," she said woodenly. "Uh, will you be…going this morning?"

Nodding slightly, he looked at her with shadowed eyes. "Yes. It's a long drive back to Texas."

She swallowed again, then nodded and rose to her feet. "Well, I'll help you get your things packed."

The moment she turned toward the house, Cordero was right behind her, his hand catching her shoulder. Slowly, her heart daring to hope, she tossed a questioning glance back at him.

"That can wait," he said. "Right now I want to—"

She waited for him to go on. When he didn't, her heart sank and she forced a smile to her face. "There's nothing else for you to say, Cordero. I'm not angry with you. Your first priority is with your family."

Yes, but *she* was beginning to feel like family, he thought. She had somehow become a part of him. And when he left for the Sandbur a piece of him would stay behind with her. He couldn't change that.

"Yes. But I thought—I was planning on the two of us having a few more days together. I wanted that, Anne-Marie. You believe that, don't you?"

She nodded and he thought he saw the glimmer of tears in her eyes. The idea made him sick, so sick that he hurt.

"Of course I believe it. We—we've had a lovely time together, Cordero. And I'm…so glad that you came, that I got to know you. You've made me open my eyes. I'm never going back to that person you first met— the woman who was running and hiding."

There was something in the middle of his chest spreading and burning, making it hard to breathe or even swallow. "I'm glad, Anne-Marie. And maybe one of these days you'll decide to come down to the Sandbur for a visit."

Her smile was tinged with sadness, as though she already knew that once he left Cane's Landing they would never see each other again.

"Who knows," she said in a strained voice. "Someday I just might surprise you."

He touched his fingertips to her cheek and wondered how his life was going to be without her, how it would be not to see her, hold her, hear her lilting voice.

He tried to smile back at her. "And maybe someday I'll find an excuse to come back to Cane's Landing."

Her blue eyes clung to his. "You might get a hankering to swim with alligators again."

He breathed deeply, hoping the extra oxygen would ease the pain in his chest. It didn't. Finally he was forced to put his hand against her back and urge her to the house.

"I'd better go pack," was all he could manage to say.

Thirty minutes later, Cordero's things were loaded in the truck and the two of them stood on the front porch steps. In the distance he could hear the first rumbles of thunder. The ominous sound matched the turmoil inside him as he turned to Anne-Marie.

"Well, uh, guess this is goodbye," he murmured.

"Don't say goodbye," she whispered. "Just say farewell."

There was such a shattered look on her face that Cordero had to pull her into his arms. For long, long moments he buried his face in her hair and held her tightly. But after a while he realized he was only prolonging the agony so he placed a soft kiss on her lips and whispered, "Farewell, Anne-Marie."

With Lucy trotting at his heels, he walked swiftly to his waiting truck. As he opened the door to climb in, the dog sat back on her haunches and whined. At the last moment, Cordero reached down and gave her an affectionate pat between the ears.

"So long, girl."

Lucy whined again, but Cordero couldn't linger. He had to leave. He had to go home and forget.

He put the truck into gear and pulled away without glancing at the house. But once he started down the long, shadowed lane he looked in the rearview mirror just long enough to see Anne-Marie standing on the steps, her hand waving a final goodbye.

Chapter Eleven

Two months later a stunned Anne-Marie walked out of the medical clinic and climbed into her car.

The doctor's diagnosis shouldn't have surprised her. In fact, for the past few weeks, she'd suspected that she might be pregnant. But hearing the actual words from her family physician had been sobering, to say the least.

What was her father going to think? Even worse, how would the local community see her? She'd already had an engagement end in disgrace. Now she would be bearing a child outside of marriage. Maybe that wasn't a big deal for many women, but to a woman who'd once planned to give her life to the church, it was scandalous. No doubt she would be branded a hussy, a fallen angel.

And yet she wanted to smile, to kick up her heels and laugh. She was going to be a mother. She was going to have Cordero's baby.

Pulling out of the parking lot, Anne-Marie drove straight to St. Mary's, where she'd been working the past two weeks helping Father Granville organize a charity function that would eventually help rebuild churches lost in Hurricane Katrina.

When she let herself into the little office at the back of the sanctuary, she found a note from the priest telling her he'd gone home to the rectory for lunch and wouldn't be back until later that afternoon.

That was probably a good thing, she thought. At least she'd have time to compose herself. As if a couple of hours could prepare her for the change her life was about to face, she thought wryly.

Tossing her handbag on a nearby table, she sat down at the desk and picked up a list of names and phone numbers of people who might be willing to work at the charity event. Father Granville expected her to make the calls, to encourage, even plead, if necessary, for the parishioners for help. But she could hardly keep her mind on the task when thoughts of Cordero attacked her from all directions.

Since he'd gone back to Texas she'd not heard from him. But then she hadn't expected to. Deep down, she'd known that he was a free spirit, a confirmed bachelor. Their time together hadn't been meant to be serious. At least, not for him.

But it is serious now, Anne-Marie. A baby is coming into the world. And Cordero is the father.

The sobering voice was rolling around and around in her head when a knock sounded on the door. The sight of her cousin Audra took Anne-Marie by total surprise. Even though she'd talked briefly with Audra several times on the phone in the past weeks, she'd not seen her since Cordero had left Cane's Landing.

Rising to her feet, she left the desk to

hurry over to the other woman. "Audra! Why are you here instead of working?"

Smiling impishly, the tall, raven-haired woman pressed a light kiss on Anne-Marie's cheek. "I'm playing hooky. We just wound up a very trying trial yesterday and I needed a break. So I told Jonas to give me a day off or get himself another secretary."

"Looks like he decided he'd better keep you happy," Anne-Marie said wryly.

She rolled her eyes. "If someone handed Jonas instructions on how to make a woman happy, he still wouldn't get it. A law book excites him more. Believe me."

For a long time now it had been obvious to Anne-Marie that her cousin was in love with her boss, but apparently he didn't see her in that manner. What surprised Anne-Marie the most about the situation was that Audra didn't boldly step forward and grab the man by the ear.

"But let's not go into that," Audra said with a dismissive wave of her hand. "I called Cane's Landing and Uncle Jules said you'd be working here today. I thought since I hadn't seen you in a couple of months I'd drop by. You've been in Thibodaux every day. Why haven't you come by the house?" she gently scolded.

The office was sparsely furnished with two metal desks and several gray metal chairs all of which had been donated to the church by a local high school. Anne-Marie gestured for Audra to take a seat.

"I've been busy," she said as she settled into a chair facing her cousin's. "And I never know when you're going to be there. You're always working late hours."

"That's the story of my life. All work and no play." Her dark eyes raked skeptically over Anne-Marie's form, which appeared even thinner than the last time Audra had seen her. "How have you been?"

Anne-Marie shrugged and found she had to let her gaze drop away from Audra's penetrating look. "Okay. I'm keeping busy. And Father likes that."

Audra shook her head with disbelief. "You know, I thought that Texas cowboy had changed you, but I guess I was wrong. You're still living your life to please others." She shook a finger at Anne-Marie. "I didn't ask you whether Uncle Jules was happy. I'm asking if you're happy."

Frowning slightly, Anne-Marie said, "Father's health is better than it's been in years. That's what I've been praying for. If he stays on this course, I can go back to Guatemala, or somewhere that I'm needed, to teach. It's what I've wanted for a long time. To finally get back to helping others."

Crossing her long legs, Audra studied Anne-Marie for long moments. "Well, I haven't had the opportunity to have a decent conversation with you since Cordero went back home. Have you heard from him?"

Trying to push away the weight of sadness inside her, Anne-Marie shook her head. "No. But then I didn't expect to."

"Why not? When I met him at the plantation I got the feeling you two were becoming pretty close."

Glancing down at her lap, Anne-Marie smoothed a finger over an invisible spot on her skirt. Audra couldn't begin to imagine how close. "Cordero lives hundreds of miles from here, Audra. There wouldn't be much point in keeping in contact."

Audra snorted. "There are such things as cars, buses, airplanes. You could be in South Texas in an hour or two."

As if that wasn't something Anne-Marie didn't think about every day. But as much as she wanted to see Cordero, needed to see him, she would never push herself on him. So what was she going to do now? How was she going to handle the news of her pregnancy? Keep it to herself? Oh God, what is the right thing for me to do, she silently prayed. Why has all of this happened to me when all I had ever planned to do was serve You?

Anne-Marie sighed. "Look, Audra, I don't know why you keep harping on Cordero. I've—"

"Maybe because he was the best thing to ever come along in your life. That's why."

Groaning with desperation, Anne-Marie rose from the chair and walked to a window that overlooked the back churchyard. The sagging branches of ancient live oaks spread deep shade across the lawn and a nearby statue of Mary, the Blessed Virgin.

Normally the peaceful scene lent Anne-Marie comfort, but today she could only wonder about the choices she'd made. At this moment they seemed all wrong. Yet she was glad, perhaps even thrilled, at the idea that this coming baby would always give her a part of Cordero. Was that wrong, too?

"Cordero is a confirmed bachelor, Audra. And I—I'm not woman enough to change him."

"How could you know that until you try?"

She had tried. In her own way. She'd given him the deepest, most precious part of herself. She'd poured out her heart to him. Maybe not in words, because she'd understood he didn't want to hear them. Still, she'd talked to him in other ways that had said *I love you*. None of it had kept him from walking away.

"You don't understand, Audra. I did try—I—" Her words choked off as emotions thickened her throat. She was ashamed at the tears slipping over the edge of her lashes. Bending her head, she wiped at the hot moisture falling onto her cheeks.

Audra placed a hand on her shoulder and squeezed. "Anne-Marie, I'm sorry. I didn't mean to upset you like this," she said gently.

Lifting her head, she looked at Audra and the concern she saw on her cousin's face only multiplied her tears.

"All right," Audra said firmly. "Something is wrong. It's the cowboy, isn't it? You fell in love with him and now you don't know what to do about it. Am I right?"

Sniffing, Anne-Marie attempted to straighten her shoulders and dry her eyes. "Yes. I did fall in love with Cordero." She shook her head in a self-deprecating way. "I'm a complete idiot, Audra."

"Don't be ridiculous! Frankly, I'm glad. I'm thrilled. For once in your life, since that fiasco with Ian, you've acted human— no, let me change that. You've acted like a woman and fell in love."

Tilting her head toward the ceiling, Anne-Marie closed her eyes with humiliation. "Yeah. With a man that I knew wasn't interested in love or marriage. I wasn't using my brain, Audra."

Her cousin chuckled. "We don't fall in love with our brains, my sweet cousin. Our hearts do it for us."

Yes, and she'd given her heart totally to Cordero. Now her love for him was producing a baby. With a helpless groan, Anne-Marie stepped around Audra and began to pace restlessly around the small office.

"You don't understand, Audra. It's more

than just falling in love with a man who doesn't want me. I'm—" Pausing, she looked across the room to where her cousin was watching her with a concerned frown. "I'm going to have Cordero's baby."

Chapter Twelve

An expression of total shock swept over Audra's face and then she ran to Anne-Marie's side, grabbing her by the shoulders.

"A baby!" she said with a gasp. "Are you sure? Maybe your cycle is just out of whack."

Shaking her head, Anne-Marie said, "I'm very certain. I just came from Dr. Layton's office less than an hour ago. He confirmed what my body was already telling me. I'm two months pregnant."

"Come here." Audra tugged on her arm

until the two of them had taken seats on the metal chairs.

Anne-Marie shot the woman an amused look. "I'm not sick, Audra. I don't need to sit down. I just need to know what I'm going to do."

Audra's dark eyes widened with disbelief. "What do you mean? You're going to have the baby, aren't you?"

Frowning with equal astonishment, Anne-Marie said, "Of course! I can't believe you would even ask that question. It's just that I don't know what to do about Cordero."

Audra shot her a droll look. "I don't see any question there. You'll tell him that he's going to be a daddy. That's the only way I see it."

Anne-Marie raked a hand through her long red hair. "Me, too," she said glumly. "And I don't think it would be right to do it over the telephone."

Audra's gaze became calculating as she studied her cousin's miserable expression. "No. You definitely need to give this sort of news in person. The man will thank you for it later."

With an unladylike snort, Anne-Marie

shot up from the chair and began to pace again. "He's not going to thank me for any of this, Audra. He has a full life. One that doesn't include a child." She slanted a glance at Audra. "I'm just going to have to reassure him that I won't hold him responsible for the child."

"What?"

The one word was flung with outrage at Anne-Marie, who passed a weary hand across her forehead and returned to the metal chair facing her cousin.

"You heard me right, Audra. Cordero didn't ask for a child. I'm not going to force one on him."

"He might not have asked for it. But he took on the consequences when he—when you two—" She broke off with a wave of her hand. "By the way, you two are grown adults. What happened to birth control?"

Scarlet color swept across Anne-Marie's cheeks as she recalled the way they'd made love under the willow on the riverbank. "We, uh, didn't have any available—but only one time."

"Apparently that was enough," Audra said wryly. "But that's beside the point. Cordero is the father. He has rights and responsibilities whether you want to deal with them or not."

Anne-Marie chewed worriedly at her bottom lip. "Yes. You're right. I have to tell him about this baby. He's the kind of man who would want to know."

Audra didn't make any sort of reply and Anne-Marie glanced over to see the other woman looking at her through misty eyes.

"What's wrong?" Anne-Marie asked. "Isn't that what you wanted to hear me say?"

Nodding, Audra gave her a wistful smile. "I was just thinking how envious I am of you. You're going to have the child of the man you love. I can't get—I can't get Jonas to even look at me."

Anne-Marie's head swung back and forth in total dismay. "Envious? You must be losing your mind, Audra. I've made a mess of my life. And I—" Her expression turned grave. "Well, I'm just glad Mama isn't alive to see it. She would be so disappointed in me."

Frowning now, Audra scolded, "Anne-Marie, once and for all I want you to quit trying to be as 'good' as your mother. She wasn't an angel or a saint. She'd be the first person to tell you that."

"No. But she wanted me to be," Anne-Marie said sadly. "And I let her down."

Audra grabbed Anne-Marie's hands and squeezed them with affection. "My sweet cousin, you were never meant to be a Sister. This is just God's way of telling you. One of these days you'll realize that."

AT THE SAME time, hundreds of miles south of Cane's Landing, Cordero was having lunch at the Cattle Call Café. Since he was a child too young to remember, he'd been eating at the little diner in downtown Goliad with his parents and siblings. It was a place where cattle buyers and horse traders gathered for coffee and blue-plate specials, even when the county livestock auction wasn't going on.

Normally Cordero loved the food and the atmosphere, but today he wasn't in the mood to listen to Chrissy Yarbrough's silly prattle. As he looked across the table at the young blonde he wondered what had ever possessed him to date her. She was like a bowl of Corn Flakes without any milk, hard to swallow.

Which wasn't saying very much for his past taste in women, he thought grimly. What had he seen in her? What had he seen in any of the girlfriends he'd had in the past few years?

Until he'd met Anne-Marie, Cordero had never asked himself such questions. He'd be the first to admit that he'd enjoyed women just for the female connection, to ease a sexual itch. Now, as he tried to tune out Chrissy's chatter, he could plainly see how shallow those brief relationships had been and he hated the fact that he'd ever had them.

He sighed and Chrissy must have picked up on his boredom because she stuck out her lower lip in a pout. "What's the matter, honey? You look all bummed out."

Cordero had to bite his tongue to keep from pointing out that she'd butted in and invited herself to his lunch table.

"Nothing, Chrissy. We've just had a lot of things going on at the ranch, that's all."

Twirling her finger around a strand of blond hair, she leaned toward him, exposing an ample portion of cleavage. "You never let that stop you from having fun before."

He frowned. "Is that all you think about? Don't you have anything productive to do?"

Since the woman had never worked a day in her life, she looked at him in comical confusion. "Why would I want to do that when Daddy has more money than I could ever spend?" Laughing, she wagged a finger at him. "Besides, what woman would want to work whenever she could play instead?"

A woman like Anne-Marie, he thought. A woman who cared for others much, much more than she cared for herself, a woman who would travel to a poor country and teach a child to read or speak English.

"Yeah, why would you?" he asked mockingly.

Chrissy scowled at him. "Cordero, you're just not acting like yourself at all. I think you need a break. Why don't you get away from the ranch this weekend?" she coyly suggested. "A bunch of us are driving down to Corpus Friday evening. I've already rented a motel room on the beach. I'd be glad to share with you."

Cordero couldn't stomach any more.

Tossing his fork onto his plate, he rose to his feet. "Sorry, Chrissy. I'm not interested. Now if you'll excuse me, I've got to get back to the ranch."

As he walked away, he could feel her throwing daggers at his back, but he was past the point of caring. She was a user.

Just like you, Cordero.

Even though he didn't want to hear the voice in his head, he couldn't ignore it. Nor could he deny it. He had used women for his own entertainment. But that was before he'd met Anne-Marie, he mentally argued as he left the Cattle Call and drove toward the Sandbur.

But you used Anne-Marie, too. You took her goodness and sweetness and left her with nothing but a goodbye.

For the remaining fifteen miles home, he tried not to think about Anne-Marie or the morning he'd told her goodbye. The memory twisted his heart to the breaking point.

He'd thought time would dim everything, even the image of her beautiful face and pale sexy body. But, if anything, the pictures in his mind seemed to grow more vivid with each passing day.

He missed her. It was that simple. And though everything inside of him wanted to call her, even drive to Louisiana and see her again, he wouldn't let himself pick up the phone, much less plan another trip to Cane's Landing. She was dangerous to his heart, his peace of mind, to everything he'd ever believed was right for himself.

It didn't matter if he was miserable without her. At least, he would never have to go through the agony of losing her as Matt had lost Erica, as his father had lost his mother.

In the dusty ranch yard at the Sandbur he pulled the truck to a stop in front of a pen used to halter-train yearlings. He'd just climbed to the ground and was about to join one of the wranglers inside the pen, when Matt's truck skidded to a dusty stop next to his. Pausing, Cordero waited for his brother to climb to the ground.

"Why the hell are you in such a hurry?" Cordero asked as dust boiled around their heads.

"I've got to get Tator saddled. Lex and I are going to ride over to pasture five to look over a herd of heifers we're thinking about selling. I'm not keen on the idea, but Lex has a buyer willing to give top dollar."

"What good is money if you don't have mama cows to produce?" Cordero retorted.

Lifting his hat from his head, Matt wiped a hand through his dark hair as he gazed thoughtfully at the western horizon. "Yeah. That's what I was thinking. I'll talk it over with Lex." He looked back at his brother, then reached inside his shirt pocket and drug out a small, velvet box. "Before I go, take a look at this. You know what women like so tell me if you think Juliet will like this. I just got back from picking it up at a jewelers in Victoria."

He popped open the box and a cluster of generous-sized diamonds winked brightly in the afternoon sunlight. The stones were fashioned in the shape of a dragonfly and Cordero suddenly wasn't seeing a piece of jewelry. He was seeing the insects swooping across the surface of the water; the river-bank where he'd first made love to Anne-Marie.

Realizing Matt was waiting for him to speak, he whistled under his breath. "You dropped a pocket of change for that bauble, big brother. Unless those diamonds are fake."

"Like hell," Matt shot back at him. "I wouldn't give Juliet fake anything."

No, Matt adored his wife and spoiled her accordingly. "What's the occasion, anyway?"

"Our second wedding anniversary," he said with a proud grin. "So what do you think? Will she like this thing? It's a pin. She's always wearing them. Up here."

He touched a spot over his left breast and Cordero was suddenly seeing his brother in a new light. Oh, it had always been clear that Matt loved his new wife, but Cordero had never really understood just what that meant or how much a woman could change a man's life. Until now. Now that Anne-Marie was living in his heart like a throbbing ember just waiting, wanting to burst into flame.

Did that mean he loved her? Maybe it did. But even admitting that didn't give him the urge to leap into marriage. Besides, Anne-Marie didn't want to be a wife. She wanted to be a missionary.

Trying to shove that dismal thought away,

Cordero slapped his brother on the shoulder. "Take my word for it, you've done good."

Grinning, Matt took off in a long stride toward the barn. Halfway there, he tossed over his shoulder. "Oh, I almost forgot. Geraldine is throwing a barbecue for us on Friday night. So don't plan on going anywhere."

Cordero gave his brother a thumbs-up sign, then turned and headed inside the yearling pen.

What the hell was Matt thinking? Was his brother blind? Cordero didn't make plans anymore. He didn't go out and have fun with his buddies anymore. He didn't do anything except brood and wonder why he didn't have the courage to take himself back to Louisiana.

Chapter Thirteen

Two days later, Anne-Marie stood outside, near the front entrance of the airport terminal with Jules at her side. In a matter of minutes she would board a flight that would take her from New Orleans to Houston. At Bush Intercontinental she would have to take a smaller commercial charter into Victoria and, from that point, rent a car to carry her on to the Sandbur.

"Are you sure you don't want me to go with you?" Jules asked for the fifth time since they'd entered the terminal. "I doubt the flight is full. I could still get a ticket."

Giving her father a grateful smile, she shook her head. "Thank you for offering, Father. But I need to do this alone."

He nodded that he understood, but Anne-Marie could see shadows of concern in his eyes. After the doctor had confirmed her condition, she'd gone home later that day and told her father about the baby.

He'd been surprised and concerned, but never once had he shown her a flicker of condemnation. She even had the feeling that he was proud of the fact that he was going to be a grandfather. Yet she could also see that he wanted things to be different for her.

"I guess you do need to do this alone," he agreed. "But I feel—well, I feel like it's my fault that you're going through all this."

"Oh, Father! You shouldn't be thinking that way. Why would you?"

Grimacing, he wiped a hand over his face. "Because I prayed to God that you and Cordero would hit it off. That you'd find the love you deserve with him."

Blinking to stem the tears burning the back of her eyes, Anne-Marie kissed his cheek. "Sometimes we're given different things than what we pray for, Father."

Jules patted the top of her head. Though he didn't speak, she could see tears of pride glistening in his eyes.

Behind her she heard people shuffling about and she glanced over her shoulder to see a skycap gathering armloads of luggage. Overhead jet engines roared, reminding Anne-Marie that her flight was near.

Forcing a smile on her face, she looked back at her father. "I'd better go check my bags. I'll see you this weekend. Audra will be here to pick me up Saturday night."

He patted her arm. "You're sure you're feeling okay?"

"I'm fine. I'll be fine." She kissed her father's cheek one last time, then turned and hurried to board the plane before he could see the tears rolling down her face.

THREE HOURS LATER Anne-Marie was driving a rental car over a rough, dusty road and wondering if somewhere along the highway, she'd taken a wrong turn. She'd not expected the drive to the Sandbur to take this long or for the big ranch to be so isolated from a town or community.

Figuring most anyone in the area would

be familiar with the huge ranch, she'd stopped at a gas station in Goliad and inquired for directions. The person had given her vague instructions with the assurance that the Sandbur was easy to find. Anne-Marie had tried to follow the mental guide in her head, but so far she'd driven for miles and miles and seen nothing but mesquite trees and some other thorny-looking underbrush. Once in a while she spotted a few white cows grazing among the desertlike vegetation, but those had been the only living things she'd seen in the past fifteen minutes.

She was about to turn around when she finally caught a glimpse of buildings in the far distance. Breathing a sigh of relief, she stepped down on the accelerator. Soon she was passing beneath an entrance made of iron pipe with a swinging weathered plank burned with the brand S/S.

The identifying mark assured Anne-Marie that she was finally on Cordero's home turf and the realization set her heart into a quick, nervous thud. What would he think when he saw her? Would he be angry that she'd invited herself to his home?

Forget those questions, you ninny, she scolded herself. The real issue would be his reaction when she told him that she was carrying his child. For the past few days she'd tried to envision how he might take her news and none of the scenarios had been good. But she couldn't let herself think about that now. If she did, she might not find the courage to face him.

Less than a quarter mile passed after the entrance when a huge, two-story hacienda-style house appeared to the right. From the descriptions her father had given her, she realized the house had to be where Cordero's aunt, Geraldine, and cousin Lex lived. The Sanchez home would be farther into the ranch on the left.

Even though it was six o'clock in the evening, the ranch appeared to be a busy place. Pickup trucks, stock trailers, tractors and baling equipment were moving about the dusty roads running between barns and feedlots. Cowboys were spreading hay and grain to horses and cattle.

As Anne-Marie's little car crawled along the dirt-packed road, she searched among the men, hoping for a glance of Cordero. But he didn't appear to be among them, which might mean he'd quit work for the day.

Moments later, she parked the car in front of a redbrick house that would have looked far more at home in her state than here in South Texas. Large white pillars supported the porch roof, which also served as a balcony for the second floor. White wooden shutters, which could be folded shut for protection from hurricanes, framed the many wide windows overlooking the front yard. Bougainvillea covered with clusters of magenta-colored blooms grew against one pillar and spread its thorny limbs along the balustrade of the balcony. Potted plants of bright yellow hibiscus sat here and there on the long concrete porch, while an iron wind chime cut in shapes of the ranch's brand tinkled in the breeze.

A stone step walkway led up to the entrance. Anne-Marie followed it until she was standing at the wide double doors. There were two golden horseshoe knockers adorning the top panels of each door, but she chose to push the doorbell to the right.

As she stood waiting for someone to answer, she realized her heart was beating uncontrollably and her palms were sweating. She had just finished wiping them down the sides of her skirt when the door pulled open and a tall, very pregnant blonde woman peered out at her.

"Hello. Can I help you?"

This had to be Juliet, Cordero's sister-in-law, Anne-Marie thought. He'd told her that she was a beautiful blonde and this woman was that and more.

Anne-Marie opened her mouth to speak and realized it was so dry she could hardly get a word out. "I—hello." Quickly, she stuck out her hand to the other woman. "I'm Anne-Marie Duveuil. I—just happened to be coming through this area and thought— I'd stop by to see Cordero."

Shaking her hand, the other woman gave Anne-Marie an easy smile. "Ms. Duveuil, how nice to meet you. You must be Jules's daughter. I'm Juliet, Matt's wife. Cordero's sister-in-law," she explained.

Releasing a tiny breath of relief, Anne-Marie smiled back at her. "I'm very pleased to meet you. And call me Anne-Marie."

Juliet stepped to one side and with a warm smile ushered Anne-Marie into the house. "Surely. And you must call me Juliet. Please come in. This is a delightful surprise."

"Thank you," Anne-Marie told her, "But let me apologize for not calling before I showed up. I wanted to surprise Cordero."

Actually, Anne-Marie had not called with her plans to visit, because Cordero would have questioned her reasons for coming and she'd not wanted to get into anything over the phone. Now she wondered if that had been a good idea. For all she knew Cordero was out of town and wouldn't be returning before she had to catch her flight back to New Orleans.

"I'm sure he's going to be thrilled," Juliet said as the two of them stepped into a large foyer filled with potted plants. "Unfortunately, he's not here right now."

Her wound nerves snapped with such sudden release that for a moment she thought her knees were going to collapse. "Oh."

Juliet glanced at her crestfallen expression and for the first time since she'd opened the door, Anne-Marie could see faint speculation in the woman's eyes.

"But don't worry, he'll be home soon,"

Juliet quickly went on. "He's in Goliad at the vet's. A horse cut his foot this afternoon and had to be operated on. If you know Cordero, you know he won't leave until he's certain the horse will be okay."

Yes, she did know how much Cordero cared about his animals. It was one of many reasons she admired him.

Anne-Marie said, "I hope the cut wasn't terribly serious."

Juliet motioned for Anne-Marie to follow her out of the foyer and into a great room. The long area was filled with comfortable leather furniture, including a couch situated in front of a wide fireplace.

"Have a seat," Juliet invited. "Anywhere you like. Would you like something to drink? Juan is making supper right now. I'm sure he has iced tea or coffee ready. Or maybe you'd like a soda?"

Trying to get into the habit of reducing her caffeine, she said, "Thank you. Water will be fine."

"Great. Just make yourself comfortable and I'll be right back."

Cordero's sister-in-law hurried out of the room. Anne-Marie eased slowly down on the edge of the couch and gazed around her. This was Cordero's home, she thought. This was where he'd laughed and talked and probably even cried with his family.

The furnishings were Western with bright Native American woven rugs on the floor and paintings of ranching scenes hanging on the wall. Footstools and magazine racks sat here and there, inviting a person to put up their feet and relax. On the wall at one end of the room was a large plasma television screen. At the moment it was turned off and the room was quiet.

From somewhere behind her, she caught the scents of cooking beef and something baking with cinnamon. She was surprised the food smells didn't jolt her stomach. For the past month any odor had left her queasy. But that malady seemed to be passing, for which she was very grateful. It would be terribly embarrassing, not to mention telling, if she had to jump up from the supper table and run to the bathroom to retch up her meal.

Her eyes returned to the fireplace in front of her, then lifted to a large oil painting hanging above the mantel. The portrait was of a young man and woman posed in a loving embrace. Anne-Marie wondered if the couple could be Cordero's mother and father and she rose to her feet to study it closer.

The woman had long dark hair flowing down her back, creamy café au lait skin with deep rosy cheeks and flashing green eyes. Anne-Marie was staring up at the beautiful face, trying to imagine her alive and mothering her sons and daughter when a footstep sounded behind her.

She turned to see Juliet reentering the room carrying a small tray of refreshments.

"Lovely portrait, isn't it?" she said as she placed the tray on the nearest end table. "That's Matt and Cordero's parents. That was done many years ago when the children were small. Elizabeth passed away a few years ago. But you probably knew that already."

Nodding, Anne-Marie glanced one last time at the portrait before she returned to her seat on the couch. "Yes. Cordero told me. He talked as though he was very close to her."

"Very." Juliet handed her a glass of ice

water, then took a seat down the couch from her. "Of course I didn't know the family back then. Matt and I have only been married for a couple of years. But my husband has told me how attached his brother was to their mother. Not to say that Matt didn't love her dearly, too. But I think there must have been a special bond between her and Cordero. Matt said that after she died Cordero quit talking. For several months he wouldn't speak at all. Just nod or shake his head. God, I'm glad I wasn't around to see that. Cordero is always such a fun-loving guy. Seeing him like that would have been hard to take. Even though, since he's come back from Louisiana he—" She broke off suddenly as though she'd caught herself before she said something she shouldn't.

Anne-Marie couldn't help but press her. "He what?"

The other woman opened her mouth to say something, but the abrupt sound of male voices coming from the foyer interrupted her.

"I don't know what the hell you expect me to do, Matt. Take the horse all the way to Texas A&M to be treated? I don't have time for that. It's not like he's the only horse on this ranch that I have to deal with."

Matt shot back at him. "Just because Tadpole isn't one of your precious cutting horses, you cart him off to that quack of a vet. Why in hell didn't you just call me about it? I would have at least taken him to Victoria!"

"He's going to be okay. So just leave it at that, will you?"

As the men's raised voices grew nearer, Anne-Marie's head turned toward the sound to see Cordero and a tall, dark man that faintly resembled him walk into the room. The brothers were so involved in their somewhat heated exchange that for a moment neither of them noticed the two women sitting on the couch.

Matt was the first to spot them and he stopped in his tracks.

"Juliet!" he exclaimed. "You didn't tell me we were having company tonight!"

Frowning, the woman rose to her feet and started toward her husband. "Too late. She's already seen you two behaving like heathens."

"Oh, honey, Cordero and I are just having

a lively discussion about vets. That's all." He met his wife halfway and leaned down to press a kiss on her cheek.

Beyond the embracing couple, Cordero stood stock-still, his gaze riveted on Anne-Marie. The stunned look on his face matched the incredible leap of her heart.

"Anne-Marie."

Even though she couldn't hear him, she could see his lips mouthing her name. Slowly, she rose on shaky legs and tried to smile as though dropping by for a visit was no big deal.

"Hello, Cordero," she said quietly.

Three long strides had him across the room and before any of them guessed his intentions he swept her into his arms and kissed her. Not just a peck on the cheek, but a full-blown kiss on her lips that rocked her all the way to her toes.

"Uh, Cordero, don't you think you should let her have some air?" Matt finally spoke up.

In spite of Matt's amused suggestion, Cordero allowed his lips to linger on Anne-Marie's before he finally lifted his head and turned a happy grin on his brother. "Matt, this is Anne-Marie. Jules's daughter."

Matt's brows shot up with surprise and then his expression turned shrewd. "Oh. So she's what it takes to put a smile back on your face."

Stepping forward, Cordero's brother offered his hand to Anne-Marie. Smiling shyly, she placed her small hand alongside the ranch manager's rough palm.

"This is a nice surprise, Ms. Duveuil," he said in greeting. "Glad you could make it to the Sandbur."

"Thank you. I'm glad to be here." She darted an uncertain glance at Cordero, who was holding her close to his side as though he wouldn't let her go. The hug of his arm warmed her, filled the gnawing emptiness she'd felt these past lonely weeks without him. "I hope my showing up out of the blue like this isn't a problem."

Cordero's face was wreathed in smiles and Anne-Marie could only wonder what his reaction meant. Had he missed her? His kiss had certainly felt as though he had. But even if he had missed her, he'd not even gone so far as to pick up the phone and dial her number.

"Are you crazy?" Cordero exclaimed. "We have plenty of room. Don't we?" He threw a questioning look at his brother and sister-in-law.

"Oh sure," Matt answered quickly. "Plenty."

"Certainly," Juliet chimed in. "The guest room is right next to Cordero's. You are planning to stay awhile, aren't you?"

Finding it safer to turn her gaze on Juliet rather than Cordero, Anne-Marie said in a hesitant voice, "Uh, I, well, I hadn't really thought about it. I'd planned to get a room in Goliad."

"Forget it," Cordero ordered. "You're not staying anywhere but here on the ranch. Let's go to your car and I'll carry in your bags."

Taking her by the hand, he tugged Anne-Marie out of the room while Matt and Juliet stared curiously after them. But once they were outside the front door and out of his family's sight, he wordlessly dragged her into his arms and covered her mouth with his.

In the back of her mind, Anne-Marie knew she should stop him, she shouldn't allow flames to rekindle between them. Not when there were so many important things she needed to discuss with him. Even so, being in his arms again, having his strong rugged body next to hers was too good to end.

Eventually, he tore his mouth from hers and pressed his cheek against the side of her hair. "Anne-Marie, I can't believe you're here," he said hoarsely. "You don't know how many times I've dreamed of this happening, but I didn't believe you would actually come."

Easing his head back from hers, he smiled at her as though he was thrilled to see her and Anne-Marie wondered sadly how soon that grin would disappear once she told him about the baby.

"How long are you going to stay? A week? Two?" he asked excitedly. "I hope you made it two. There are so many things I want to show you here on the ranch, so many places to take you and things for us to do."

"Cordero, I—" She paused, not knowing what to say next. She didn't want to get to the crux of the matter out here. Especially when she figured it was almost suppertime. No, Cordero would have to learn about the baby later, when they could have total privacy.

"Oh, don't bother answering that now," he went on in a dismissive way. "I won't let you leave, no matter what you say." Dimples creased his cheeks as his twinkling gaze traveled up and down her slim figure. "Gosh, you look beautiful. So beautiful."

His enthusiasm at seeing her again was infectious and Anne-Marie told herself to simply relax and enjoy these precious moments before this peaceful time with him ended.

Smiling back at him, she said, "You look pretty good yourself."

With a mocking laugh, he looked down at his denim Western shirt and faded blue jeans. "Yeah. Dust and horse manure is the new fashion. Not to mention dried blood." He grabbed her hand again and headed toward the car she'd left parked in the graveled driveway. "Let's get your bags and get back in. I need a few minutes to clean up for supper."

He was taking it for granted that she'd simply come to the Sandbur to spend time with him. And he was happy about it. Very happy. The whole idea made her want to weep.

Careful to hide her unease, she followed him to the car.

Back in the house, Cordero quickly excused himself and headed to the shower while Juliet took Anne-Marie upstairs to the guest room.

"No one has stayed in here since Matt and Cordero's sister, Lucita, came to stay a couple of months ago during their cousin's wedding. I hope everything has been straightened," she said as she pushed open the door to the bedroom and flipped on the light.

Anne-Marie followed her inside the spacious room and gazed curiously around her. She could see a flavor of the Sanchez's Western lifestyle in the iron bedstead, varnished pine armoire and matching dresser. A row of rusty spurs and sweat-stained cowboy hats hung from pegs along one wall.

Sepias depicting cattle drives and bronco-
busters, along with actual family photos,
adorned the remaining walls.

A handmade quilt done in a wedding ring
pattern covered the bed. Her leather traveling bag was sitting near the pillows where
Cordero had left it. The sight of the bag reminded her of when she'd awkwardly shown
Cordero to his bedroom at Cane's Landing.
Only nine weeks had passed since then, but
the agony she'd gone through had seemed
like a lifetime. Would her suffering end now
or only deepen?

"This is lovely. I'm sure everything will
be fine." She turned to the other woman.
"And I apologize again for showing up so
unexpectedly. I realize you're all very busy
and—"

"Don't think a thing about it," Juliet interrupted with a wave of her hand, then with a
little grin, she stepped closer and lowered
her voice to a conspiring tone. "Actually,
now that the men aren't around, I wanted
to say—I'm really, really glad you showed
up. Cordero has been a growling bear ever
since he came back from Louisiana. Tonight
when he walked through the door and saw

you, it was like seeing a light switched on. I was finally seeing the Cordero I know and love. You're exactly what he needed."

Anne-Marie wanted to burst into tears. "Juliet, if you're thinking that Cordero is in love with me or something like that—you couldn't be more wrong. He, uh—"

"Don't try to explain. I understand that Cordero doesn't believe he'll ever be bitten by the love bug. But what do men know about it? Matt swore he'd never marry again, but now he has me and a baby on the way. Sometimes we women just have to give them the right sort of nudge to open their eyes."

Wondering how she could possibly reply to Juliet's observations, Anne-Marie was faintly relieved when the sound of Matt's voice suddenly called up to them.

"Juliet, can you come here for a minute?"

Rolling her eyes, Juliet grinned and held up her palms in a helpless gesture. "See, the man can't do without me." She started out the door, then tossed over her shoulder, "Hurry down and I'll show you around the house before we eat."

The tension of the past few minutes had

taken its toll on Anne-Marie and once Juliet had left the room, she closed the door and sank onto the edge of the bed. Her hands were shaking and emotional tears burned her eyes. She'd known that seeing Cordero again and telling him about the baby was going to be a difficult task. But she'd not anticipated how crushing it was going to feel to meet his family and know that she would never be a part of them.

Chapter Fourteen

As usual, supper for the Sanchez family was a lively affair with conversation and laughter flowing around the dining table. With Anne-Marie present, the occasion had even taken on a festive air, but this was one meal Cordero was itching to see end.

He had to get Anne-Marie alone. Making love to her warred with the urge to talk to her, to find out why she'd really shown up here at the Sandbur. She'd told Juliet that she'd just happened to be in the area, but he didn't believe that for one minute. She'd come to see him. But why? Because she desperately missed him, or was she merely accepting his invitation to visit the ranch?

Cordero was so preoccupied with the questions he didn't notice when his family finally began to make noises about leaving the table and adjourning to the great room for coffee. When he did, he scraped back his chair and reached for Anne-Marie's arm.

"Sorry folks, but you're going to have to drink it without us. I want some time alone with Anne-Marie."

Cordero's blunt statement brought a stare of surprise from Matt, while their father smiled knowingly down at his plate. It was Gracia, Matt's teenage daughter who relieved the awkward silence.

"Gee, Uncle Cordero, I didn't know you could be romantic. Why don't you take her out to the gazebo? You can smell the lilac from there."

Cordero winked at his niece. "Good idea, funny face. Thanks."

Frowning now, Matt jerked his head toward his daughter. "Since when do you know anything about romance? You're just a kid."

Throwing back her shoulders, Gracia

wiggled to the tallest posture she could manage. "Have you forgotten, Daddy? I'm fourteen now!"

Matt banged the heel of his hand against his forehead with feigned realization. "Oh, how could I forget? You're practically in adulthood now."

Smiling to herself at the father-daughter interplay, Anne-Marie allowed Cordero to lead her out of the dining room and through a long hallway.

"That might go on for hours," Cordero said with amusement as he ushered her through a back door. "Gracia's at the age where she wants to be taken seriously. And she is grown-up enough to know what's on my mind."

But he had no idea what was on hers, Anne-Marie thought dismally, and that was something she was going to have to change, and quickly. The secret she carried was tormenting her to the point of physical illness.

Her stomach churned, her heart pounded as his arm slid around her shoulders and guided her across grass so thick that her feet felt as though they were sinking into carpet.

Twenty feet away, a gazebo covered with

some sort of trailing vine was tucked beneath two pine trees. Footlights circled the lattice board siding and lit the way up the steps. The minute Cordero helped her onto the planked floor of the private shelter, he spun her into the circle of his arms and bent his head toward hers.

Knowing she couldn't explain anything with him kissing her senseless, she placed a hand in the middle of his chest and tried to wedge a space between them.

"Wait, Cordero. I need to talk to you."

Lifting his head, he looked down at her with bemusement. "I want to talk to you, too, Anne-Marie. But do you know how much I've missed you? How much I want to make love to you?"

Just hearing him say he'd missed her should have filled her with gladness, but it wasn't enough. She wanted to hear he needed her, that he would love her always. But she knew better than to expect those sorts of words from him.

"I—yes. I think I do," she said huskily. "But—"

He suddenly interrupted her. "Why did you really come here, Anne-Marie? I know I invited you, but you didn't make any promises about coming to the ranch. I got the feeling that you would probably never come."

Bending her head, she tried to summon the courage to utter the words that she'd traveled all the way to Texas to say. "You were right. I had no intention of coming here. Because I understood what happened between us was over. And I—" she looked up at him. "To be honest, telling you good-bye was too painful to think about going through again."

Groaning, he clamped his hands around her upper arms. "So what made you change your mind? If you didn't want to see me again—"

"I had to," she blurted desperately, then went on before she could stop herself. "Because I—because I'm going to have your baby."

He stared at her in stunned silence as moment after moment ticked by. Anne-Marie could only wonder at the questions and images going through his mind.

"A baby," he finally whispered. "You're pregnant? For sure?"

Glad that she'd finally released the news, she nodded. "Very. My doctor says the baby will be here in late March or early April."

With dazed movements, he released his hold on her and sank onto a portion of the bench that outlined the interior of the gazebo. "A baby," he whispered again as though the word was strange and he needed to practice saying it. "This changes everything."

Her knees were so weak and shaky that she was forced to sink down beside him. "Yes. There's no denying that," she said in a strained voice.

His head swung back and forth. "I'm sorry, Anne-Marie. I shouldn't have behaved so recklessly that day at the river. At the time I couldn't think for wanting you. Then later, we used protection and I pretty much dismissed that one time. Guess it's true that one time is all it takes."

She looked at him and as her eyes glided over his dark profile all the yearning she felt for the child growing inside her seemed to multiply tenfold.

"No need to be sorry, Cordero. It just happened. But don't worry. I can deal with it."

His head reared back. "*You* can deal with it? Don't you mean *we?*"

Bracing herself, she shook her head. "No. I mean you can exercise your fatherly rights if you want to, but I fully intend to raise this baby myself."

He looked at her as though she'd lost her mind. "Exercise my fatherly rights? What kind of talk is that? This isn't the same Anne-Marie I got to know two months ago!"

She pursed her lips and tried to steel herself against the pain cracking her heart. "I'm not that same Anne-Marie. I'm pregnant. That makes a woman see everything differently."

"Different, hell!" he snorted. "You'd better get to seeing them clearly. Because your way is *not* the way it's going to be."

Anne-Marie was suddenly reminded that the Sanchez's were a rich, prominent family. If Cordero was of a mind to, he could give her a whale of a fight over the baby's custody. She'd never for once believed he might resort to something like that, but now fear was spreading icy fingers throughout her body.

"What do you mean?"

He reached for her hand and as his fingers tightened around hers, she wanted nothing more than to throw herself into his arms and weep.

"It means our child is going to grow up in the normal way. With a mother and father living in the same house."

The implication of his words staggered her. Her eyes widened; her jaw fell. "Are you suggesting marriage?"

"Why yes. That's the way I see it."

Jumping from the bench, she turned her back to him and bit down hard on her lip. Why now, she wondered sickly. Why couldn't he have asked her to marry him before she'd stood on the steps of Cane's Landing with her heart breaking as she'd waved a final goodbye?

Because he hadn't wanted to marry you then, Anne-Marie. No more than he really wants to marry you now. This is all about the baby. Nothing more.

"You can put that out of your head," she whispered firmly, "because I have no intention of marrying you."

Shooting up from the bench, he moved up behind her and clamped his hands over her shoulders. "I don't believe I'm hearing you right."

His arrogant reply had her whirling on him and pride sharpened her words. "Why? Because you think you're such a prince you can't imagine any woman turning you down? Well, let me give you a news alert, this woman is saying no!"

Lifting his face toward the vine-covered roof of the gazebo, he sighed with heavy frustration. "Anne-Marie, I don't understand this—you! This isn't about you or me! It's about our baby and what's best for him!"

Her features hardened. "You think you have to point that out to me? I understand you completely, Cordero. But that isn't going to sway my decision. In the long run, entering into a marriage that I don't want would be disastrous for the child."

His gaze was like a razor, dissecting every inch of her face as though he was trying to discover something that just wasn't there. "Anne-Marie, I thought I knew you. I thought you were different. I thought you were a woman who would always put others before yourself. What has happened to

you? Is this what you think God wants you
to do? Raise the baby without a father?"

Stunned that he would resort to such a
low blow, she said in a fierce rush, "Don't
question my faith, Cordero. You can't see
inside my heart. When I lay down in the
grass with you, you didn't understand why.
And you still don't!"

With a painful sob, she stepped around
him and hurried back to the house.

He caught her before she reached the door
and as his big hand grasped her shoulder,
she stood frozen, staring into the darkness
as tears rolled down her face.

"Maybe I am just a callous ranch hand,"
he muttered roughly. "But that doesn't mean
I can't feel. That baby inside you is mine.
And I want to make sure he's raised right.
With a father in the house—his real father!"

"That's quite something coming from
you, Cordero. When not more than two
months ago you insisted you never wanted
to get married."

He growled in frustration and Anne-Marie realized she'd never been this nasty to
anyone. Why was she lashing out at him
like this? It wasn't right to punish him just

because he didn't love her. That was something she'd been perfectly aware of when she'd given herself to him. Now it was too late for anger or indignation.

"I'm sorry I said that, Cordero. I'm not being fair. And maybe I'm not behaving like myself, either." Her eyes were full of regret as she turned her head toward his. "I need to rest. I've had a terribly long day. We'll talk about all this tomorrow."

Dropping his hand from her shoulder, he reached to open the door. "All right. The last thing I want to do is tire you out. But this is not over, Anne-Marie. Not by a long shot."

No, it was just beginning, she thought dismally, and if the next few days were anything like this one, she didn't see how she could bear up under the stress.

Once they were back in the great room, Anne-Marie quickly excused herself and hurried up to her bedroom.

From his seat in an armchair, Matt looked at his brother with faint amusement. "That sure didn't last long. You must be losing your touch, little brother."

"Shut up, Matt. Just shut the hell up!" Cordero growled, then stalked out of the room before anyone else had a chance to say another word to him.

THE NEXT MORNING Cordero left the house long before sunrise. A horse buyer was scheduled to meet him at seven and Cordero needed to have the animals saddled and warmed up long before the man arrived.

Earlier, Matt had helped him drive a small herd of heifers into the cutting pen and now, with the buyer watching, Cordero was demonstrating the ability of the last filly he had for sale.

Beneath him he could feel the chestnut filly's muscles bunch then surge with incredible power. Dirt flew from her hooves and rained on his hat like chunks of hail in a violent rainstorm. Her ears were laid flat against her head, her teeth bared as she watched and outmaneuvered the heifer trying to get past her.

Horse and rider were in the zone. That place where the dance was perfect and it felt as though they were both floating in unison. Normally Cordero lived for these moments. There was nothing more exhilarating than riding a cutting horse, using every ounce of strength and balance he had to stay in the saddle. But this morning the joy was dimmed and he had little patience for the buyer when, a few minutes later in the ranch office, he began to sputter about the price.

"Look, Manning," Cordero said from behind a messy desk piled with papers, foam cups and pieces of tack that hadn't yet found their way back to the barn. "Sweet Pea is my favorite filly. She's only three, but she performs as well or better than a ten-year-old. I don't have to sell her. In fact—" he propped his elbows on the desk and leaned toward the horse buyer "—I've changed my mind. She's not for sale. And she won't ever be."

"But we're only talking about five hundred dollars difference here, Cordero," the man began to argue.

"Forget it. She's mine. She's gonna stay mine," he said bluntly.

Sensing he was on a slippery slope, the buyer didn't argue further and quickly wrote out a check for the horses the two of them had already agreed upon.

Ten minutes later, the door to the small office had barely closed behind Manning when Matt stepped in.

Looking at his brother, Matt motioned behind him. "I just met Manning on the way to his truck. He looked like a mad hornet. What happened? He didn't buy any horses?"

Cordero slapped a copy of the receipt into the bottom drawer of the metal desk. "Three. And he was lucky to get them. He wanted me to cut the price on Sweet Pea. Damn idiot! Even a kid could see she's the best one in the lot. That's why he wanted to steal her."

Matt lips formed a silent *O* as he studied his brother's thunderous expression. "I'm afraid to ask what you told him."

Cordero rose to his feet. "I wasn't rude, if that's what you're worried about. Well, maybe not too much." He realized he was behaving out of character but he couldn't seem to do anything about it. Everything inside of him felt pushed and pulled and twisted until he didn't know where to turn or what to do to find relief. "I just told him that Sweet Pea was mine and I've decided to take her completely off the market."

"Oh." Matt nodded and stepped over to a coffeemaker and a stack of foam cups. "Just not quite in those words though, right?"

"No. I don't think I used that many," he said grimly.

Matt took his time pouring himself a cup of coffee before he turned back to Cordero.

"Well, that's your prerogative," he said amiably. "The filly is yours to keep."

"Damn right," Cordero muttered, then walked across the room to a plate glass window that overlooked the cutting pen.

Two Sandbur wranglers were unsaddling the horses that Manning had purchased. It eased him to see Sweet Pea still tied to a hitching post and he realized he never should have put the filly up for sale in the first place. She'd been born on the ranch to a Sandbur mare and since she'd been a tiny colt she'd followed Cordero around like a faithful dog. She was smart and beautiful, but more importantly, she was all heart. She gave him her best, always. And she'd quietly endeared herself to him.

Just as Anne-Marie had.

"Uh, you gonna knock off the rest of the day?"

Matt's question had Cordero turning away from the window. "I don't know. Why?"

"Why?" Matt asked with amazement. "You have company, remember?"

Company. Anne-Marie wasn't company. She was his whole world. Back at Cane's Landing when he'd stood in the rose garden and told her he'd had to leave, some inexplicable essence had kept whispering to him that he loved her. That he was meant to spend his life with her. But he'd not wanted to heed the voice inside his head or admit to himself the he'd actually fallen in love. Maybe if he'd faced his feelings then, Anne-Marie wouldn't be refusing to marry him now.

"Yeah," he said sardonically. "I remember."

Matt frowned. "Cordero, I'm sick and damned tired of handling you with gloves. Now what's the problem? Are you mad at Anne-Marie for showing up here at the ranch? If you don't care about the woman then you need to tell her how it is and send her on her way!"

"Don't be telling me what to do! Especially when you don't know anything about it," Cordero said in an angry blast.

Not about to back down, Matt stalked

over to his brother. "Then maybe you'd better tell me how it is. Because I'm not going to put up with you biting my head off!"

Cordero opened his mouth to snarl out a curse word, then at the last moment snapped it shut. Matt was right. He had to get a grip. He had to go back to the house, face Anne-Marie and convince her that he was a man worth marrying.

Wiping a hand over his face, he said, "I'm sorry, Matt. I know I've been behaving like a jackass, but I'm—" He paused, heaved out a heavy sigh, then blurted, "Anne-Marie is pregnant with my child. She came here to the ranch to tell me."

Matt's expression didn't falter, but Cordero knew that he'd stunned his brother. He didn't say anything for long moments, just looked at him as though he was trying to gauge Cordero's feelings about the matter.

"And that has you angry?" he asked.

Pain flickered inside Cordero's chest, then took hold and spread upward until his throat was thick. "Not about the baby. I'm upset because—because she won't marry me."

"Oh. Why not?"

Cordero's arms lifted and fell in a helpless gesture. "I wish I knew. I thought—" He stopped and shook his head in anguish. "Maybe I was arrogant to assume she would want to marry me. Maybe I went at everything all wrong. I don't know."

Matt looked at him with wry speculation. "You mean you sorta made it an order instead of a marriage proposal?"

Cordero's eyes slanted sheepishly up to meet his brother's. Matt always seemed to know him better than he knew himself. "Yeah. Sorta. But I was shocked at the time. And I—want that baby, Matt. I want it with all my heart."

Stepping forward, Matt placed a comforting hand on Cordero's shoulder. "And what about Anne-Marie?" he asked gently.

Matt's question released the pain twisting inside of Cordero's chest and he found it a relief to answer his brother. "I want her just as much."

Matt's fingers squeezed around his shoulder. "Then you need to make that clear to her."

Nodding with sudden hope, Cordero headed toward the door and jerked it open.

"Yeah, you're right, brother. I need to start all over. I need a ring and roses and—"

"To hell with that!" Matt called after him. "She doesn't want a ring or roses. She wants your love."

"She'll get that, too!" Cordero tossed back at him, then hurriedly stepped out of the office.

BACK AT THE Sanchez house Anne-Marie had slept shamefully late and now descended the stairs to find the house quiet and everyone seemingly gone to work. As she neared the kitchen, she could hear the faint sounds of a radio playing country music and expected to find the Sanchez cook when she entered the room. Instead, she found Cordero's father, Mingo, pouring water into a coffeemaker.

He was a massively built man with broad shoulders and big hands. Except for a white streak running along the right side of his head, his hair was thick and black and curled around his head in an extremely attractive way. She could see a resemblance to Cordero in his face and strong build, but even more so in the man's charming smile.

"Good morning," he greeted. "I'm glad

you made it up. I was beginning to worry that you were sick."

A small kitchen table was located at one end of the room. She pulled out one of the chairs and sank into it. "Oh. I apologize for sleeping so late. This isn't like me at all. I hope you haven't been waiting on me."

Smiling, Mingo shook his head. "It's never a bother to wait on a beautiful woman." He glanced at the coffeemaker, then opened one of the cabinet doors. "Would you like coffee? It's decaffeinated—just in case you might be worried about that."

Anne-Marie's eyes darted over to Mingo's back. Had Cordero told his father about their baby? Or had the wise man made his own deductions about her sudden appearance here on the Sandbur? Either way, the idea that he might know she was pregnant with his son's child was enough to put a rosy blush on her cheeks.

"I would love some," she told him. "Thank you."

He set a steaming mug in front of her, then placed a tiny pitcher of cream and a sugar bowl on the table. She stirred in a hefty dollop of cream as Mingo went over to a large gas range and opened the oven.

"Juan left breakfast tacos for you. There's egg and bacon. Egg and sausage. Or egg, bacon and potato."

He carried a platter loaded with tacos wrapped separately in aluminum foil over to the table and set it down within Anne-Marie's reach.

"All these!" she exclaimed. "There's enough food here for an army!"

Mingo chuckled. "We have lots of eaters around here. And two of them don't want to fix things for themselves at lunchtime, so they grab these when there're some left over."

She figured the two he was talking about were Cordero and his brother, Matt. Juliet had told her last night before the evening meal that she worked at a local newspaper and would be out of the house today until six.

Smiling in spite of her aching heart, she reached for one of the tacos. "Well, I'm glad your cook didn't have to go to extra trouble for me. I feel like I'm intruding upon your family."

Mingo batted a hand through the air. "Nonsense. We're happy that you're here."

She heaved out a heavy sigh as she unwrapped the taco. "Well, I'm not so sure Cordero was that pleased to see me."

He chuckled again. "I hardly think that's true. Matt said Cordero gave you such a bear hug he nearly broke your ribs."

Yes, but that was before she'd told him about the baby. That was before he'd insisted the two of them had to marry, she thought grimly. Insisted. Ordered. Demanded. In all of her dreams, she'd never expected a man to propose marriage to her in such a way. The memory of it still left her stinging with humiliation.

She bit into the soft flour tortilla and scrambled egg and was relieved when her stomach didn't revolt.

"Cordero is a busy man. I don't expect him to leave his work undone to cater to me. In fact, I think I should leave this afternoon."

"Now why would you want to do that? You just got here."

Because Cordero didn't want her here. Not really. Oh, he'd been excited when he'd first spotted her all right. But everything had still been fun and games to him then. The second he'd heard about the baby, he'd turned into a bear. Complete with fangs. The only thing he was interested in now was the baby and how it would ultimately be raised.

"I just think it would be better."

"For you? Or for Cordero?"

She swallowed as her throat thickened with emotion. "Both, I suppose."

Suddenly Mingo's hand reached across the table and covered hers. "Anne-Marie, I don't think it's as bad as you think it is."

She had to bite her lip to keep from groaning out loud. "You just don't know, Mr. Sanchez."

His big fingers patted the back of her hand. "I'm not Mr. Sanchez to you. I'm Mingo. And yes, I think I do know. I knew something was different the minute Cordero got back from Louisiana. The boy has been pining for you. And it's good that you came."

Close to tears now, Anne-Marie bent her head. "I should have never gotten involved with him. He—he's not a marrying sort of man."

With a heavy sigh Mingo rose from the table. Anne-Marie lifted her head to watch him quietly pour himself a mug of coffee, then carry it back to the table.

He said, "You know I met Jules when he came to buy that pair of grays from Cordero. I liked him. Liked him a lot. We're birds of a feather, your father and me."

Puzzled by his comment, she studied the older man's face. Mingo was a tough outdoorsman, where her father ran the plantation from a business end. Mingo was built like a bull and just as robust, while her father was tall and slender with frail health. As far as she could tell the two men couldn't have been more opposite.

"What do you mean?" Anne-Marie asked him.

"We both lost our wives way too soon to suit us."

"Oh." The shadows in his eyes were too painful for her to take in and she dropped her gaze away from him to the tabletop. "Yes, Cordero told me about losing his mother."

"That tore him right in two," Mingo replied. "You see, we've had a lot of loss here on the Sandbur. Only a few months before Elizabeth died, Matteo lost his first wife, Erica, in a riding accident. In fact, she was a lot like you—red hair and very beautiful. When we had her funeral Elizabeth was still well enough to stand at her graveside. But she was frail and losing ground even then."

He drew in a deep breath and let it out before he spoke again. "When she slipped away, it was the breaking point for Cordero. He was like a dog trying to lick his own wounds and growling if anyone tried to help him. He swore to me that he'd never marry. That he was never going to go through the hell his father and brother had gone through. I told him that he was wrong—that Elizabeth would be ashamed of him. But he wouldn't listen. Since then I've been praying that time would heal him. Or maybe a woman like you."

Anne-Marie's eyes slipped back to Mingo's face and she was surprised to see that he was smiling. Here was a man who'd come close to losing his life in a violent way. Even now his voice held the faint hint of a slur, the corner of his mouth stretched unnaturally downward. Yet in spite of all the trials he'd endured, he was still a happy man. And suddenly she was ashamed of her self-pity, of putting her own wants first instead of the needs of her child and the man that she loved.

She was trying to collect herself enough to speak when Mingo added, "Anne-Marie, there are some people that seem to breeze through life without a care and die old in their bed. But God seems to put trials on those that love him the most. To test us. Teach us. You'll make it through this trial, Anne-Marie. You and Cordero."

As Mingo's words sank in, she realized again how wrong she'd been to lash out at Cordero last night. She'd wanted to punish him for not giving her what she wanted. She'd even been angry with him for not understanding her needs when all along she should have been telling him what was really in her heart.

Give and you shall receive. It was time she followed those instructions.

"Where is Cordero this morning?" she asked.

"He's down at the cutting pen. If you want to go, I'll drive you," he offered with a grin.

Rising from her seat, she skirted the table and hugged Cordero's father. "Thank you," she whispered.

He patted her shoulder and then she straightened away from him and smiled with a gratefulness that glowed in her blue eyes.

"Just let me go change into a pair of boots and I'll be ready," she told him.

He nodded. "I'll wait here for you."

Her heart suddenly lifting with renewed spirit and hope, she left the kitchen and hurried up the staircase to her bedroom.

She had placed her bag on the foot of the bed and was digging through the contents in order to reach her boots when a knock sounded on the door.

Figuring Mingo had followed her up to tell her something else, she called, "Come in."

"What are you doing? Packing to leave?"

Cordero's voice stunned her and she whipped around to see him striding into the room. There was a look of stark fear on his face as his gaze took in her and the bag and the idea suddenly struck her that he'd lived these past years refusing to love, dreading he would lose again.

"Cordero, I thought—" Her heart hammering, she stepped toward him. "I'm not packing. I came up here for my boots. Your father was going to drive me to the cutting pen, to see you."

The tight grimace on his face eased. "I had to leave the house early this morning. I'm sorry about that. I know we need to talk and—"

Love swelled inside her chest and she didn't try to stop herself from showing it as she went to him and gathered his hands within hers. "Cordero, before you say anything, let me say this. I was wrong last night. I shouldn't have lashed out at you. This isn't all about me."

His eyes were skeptical as they roamed her face. "I don't care if you're angry with me. Slap me. Kick me. Whatever you have to do. I just want to know why you don't want to marry me?" He moved close enough to touch her face and as his fingers trailed down her cheek so did her tears.

"Because I—" She stopped, then started over. "I don't want you to marry me because you feel it's the right thing to do. I want you to marry me because you love me—me and the baby. But if that isn't possible—"

Her words broke off as he swiftly circled his arms around her shoulders and pulled her tight against him. "Oh, Anne-Marie," he said in a choked voice, his face buried in the side of her hair. "You don't have to explain more. Because I know now that you love me."

Rearing her head back, she looked up at him with bemusement. "Does that part matter?"

He suddenly chuckled and the sound was like music, assuring her heart that everything was going to be as it should be.

"It's only everything." He lifted his hands to frame her face. "I think I've been in love with you from the first moment I saw you walking across the yard at Cane's Landing. I just didn't want to admit it to myself. I didn't want to think that I could need anyone that much—that I would ever put myself into such a vulnerable place. But these past two months without you have been a living hell for me. Even if you hadn't shown up to tell me about the baby, deep down, I knew I was going to have to go to you."

Shaking her head with wonder, she smiled at him through misty tears. "Why didn't you tell me this last night?"

Groaning with regret, he stroked his hand down the back of her hair. "Because I'm a stubborn man, Anne-Marie. This morning I got into it with a horse buyer. I was fuming because he tried to get me to lower the price on a filly I had for sale. I wound up telling him to forget the whole thing, that I would never sell her. And then after the man left the ranch, I realized I wasn't really angry with him. Lots of buyers try to negotiate the price. I was actually mad at myself for putting Sweet Pea up for sale in the first place. I loved her and deep down I didn't want to lose her. It's the same with you, my darlin'. I love you and I don't want to lose you. Will you marry me, Anne-Marie? Be my wife for as long as we both shall live?"

She let out a soft sigh of joy as he lifted her hand to his lips. "Cordero, I love you. I wanted to be your wife long before I learned about the baby. I think—well, for a long time, I was hanging on to a dream, trying to be the perfect angel my mother often called me. Trying to live up to what I thought she wanted me to be wasn't the right reason to enter a convent." She shook her head and smiled with awe. "Thankfully there was a higher hand guiding me toward you."

His eyes full of love, he slipped his arms around her waist and cradled her against him. "I understand your need to help others, Anne-Marie, and after we're married I want you to continue to do that. Just so your work doesn't take you too far away from me and our children."

She slid her palms up his broad chest, then cupped them around the sides of his face. "Maybe you did understand me when I lay down with you in the grass," she said softly.

Smiling, he lowered his lips to hers. "You were giving me your heart. And now it's too late to take it back. I plan on keeping it forever."

He sealed his promise with a lengthy kiss that had Anne-Marie's heart singing, shouting, rejoicing.

When he finally lifted his head, she said,

"Mingo is waiting down in the kitchen. Maybe we'd better go give him the news that he's getting a new daughter-in-law."

Laughing, Cordero grabbed her by the hand and led her out of the room. "We'll go tell him. But somehow I don't think it will be news to him."

TEN MONTHS LATER on an early spring day filled with bright sunshine, Joseph Cordero Sanchez was christened at the family church not far from the Sandbur, then whisked home to a house full of family and friends gathered for the celebration.

As always on the Sandbur, a party required lively music, plenty of good food, with equal amounts of dancing. All three were presently in such full force that some of the merrymaking had spilled into the backyard and even down to the barns.

Little Joseph was the second baby to be born to the Sanchez family in the past few months. He joined Matt and Juliet's son, Jess, who was born a week before Christmas. Both boys had been ruling the household and today were getting equal attention as adults fawned and cooed over the two little cousins.

Jules, who seemed to be getting stronger and healthier every day, had traveled down from Louisiana to attend his grandchild's baptism. At the moment he and Mingo had withdrawn to a corner of the great room and were conspiring to slip out of the house and down to the horse barn.

At the opposite end of the room, near the staircase landing, Cordero's sister, Lucita, stood with their Aunt Geraldine, watching the celebration.

"I'm so glad you and Marti could drive up from Corpus to be here today," Geraldine told her. "This day means so much to Cordero and Anne-Marie."

Lucita's eyes drifted over to her two brothers, who were both holding their baby sons, showing them off to friends with fatherly pride. The sight was a very happy one. Yet it also filled her heart with sadness. Her son was without a father now. The man had disappeared from their lives. But not before trying to hurt her in every possible way.

"I'm glad I could come," she said to Ger-